Praise for Tsipi Keller

Praise for *Jackpot*

Keller, then, is bilingual when it comes to the discourse of emotion: she understands both the language of bland social accommodation and the language of excessive despair. The former shouts at us like an alibi, jarring in its cheerfulness. The latter is inarticulate and sulking and overcomes us in its morbid embrace. It's as if this book were written both by a Henry James and a Hubert Selby, Jr.: a glittering chronicler of social mores, where exterior and interior worlds interweave a rich tapestry, and a poète maudit, who savors the most abject and perverse treasures of the human condition.

Bruce Benderson/The Brooklyn Rail

Tsipi Keller's *Jackpot* reminds me of Jean Rhys like no book I've read in years. I love Rhys; that's high praise. It's also a consumer warning: This book is a study in self-destruction. It's addictive, intense—a psychological page-turner that doesn't miss a beat. It's sexy as hell. But, for readers who like their fiction as crisply edged as their lawns, it's much too disturbing for the beach or daily commute… And when it's over? Maggie's in a zone you wouldn't have predicted. And so are you. Proof, I'd say, of an exceptional work of fiction.

Jesse Kornbluth/HeadButler.com

This marvelously engaging and pleasurable novel is like a cross between watching a sly Eric Rohmer film about the spiritual crisis of vacation and reading a Jean Rhys interior monologue of a woman in extremis. For all its horrific aspects, it has a steady undercurrent of humor: the comedy derives from showing the precise mechanisms of low self-esteem, rationalization and self-indulgence. A wickedly readable, psychologically astute and drolly knowing fiction.

Phillip Lopate

The problem with novels of degradation is that the depressing nature of the narrative slows down the reading. If you like the character, then you'll not like seeing the character take a trip down the big swirly. Keller gets the reader past this with her present-tense prose and the wealth of understated humor inherent in her perspective on her character...

The publisher of Keller's novel, Spuyten Duyvil, is not exactly a household name, but they have a huge line of original fiction available in these attractive trade paperback editions.

Rick Kleffel/Agony Column

The original literary characters to be obsessed by what proved to be a false paradise from which they felt excluded, and who found what they thought was a neat short-cut which ended up taking them in the opposite direction, were Milton's Adam and Eve. The imaginative brilliance of *Jackpot* is reflected in its ability to reveal and make new this archetypal pattern, while seeming to focus so relentlessly and exclusively on the here and now immediacy of Maggie and her small world. This is an extraordinary achievement, made even more so by the extent to which it seems hidden, at first, within the fabric of the book's compelling realism and accessibility.

Andrew Kaufman

It isn't very long before you realize that Keller has caught you in a deceptive web of shallow ideals and insanity that in no way resemble the bland Ally McBeal psycho-babble you were prepared for. As a matter of fact it's closer to the ever-descending rings of hell of Hubert Selby's *Requiem for a Dream*. Unlike the intensity of Selby's work, Keller's story has a hypnotic, seductive quality that pulls the reader further into Maggie's escalating disintegration.

Paul McDonald/Louisville Courier Journal

I guess you could call *Jackpot* a beach read's worst nightmare, in the best possible sense: sun, sand, and palm trees cannot begin to mask the dark corners of this paradise.

Robert Gray/Fresh Eyes

Tsipi Keller's new novel *Jackpot* is a skillfully plotted story of a character's unraveling, so gradual and inexorable that you move from comfort level to comfort level without realizing how uncomfortable you're getting, like the proverbial frog in the pot... One thinks, oddly enough, of *The House of Mirth*. Though Maggie doesn't have to fall as far as Lily Bart, she falls in the same curious stepwise fashion... One thinks, too—continuing the theme of the American fallen-woman novel—of *The Awakening*, but *Jackpot* is very much a postmodern fallen-woman novel, without any of the moral and social anxieties that characterize even as modernist a work *as The Awakening*.

Tim Morris/Lection

Jackpot is a wonder of a book. It is irresistibly fascinating—painfully fascinating. You may not feel like sharing the experiences of its misguided heroine, but you should, because you'll have a livelier time sticking with her than to your own comfortable ways. And you can always reassure yourself that you'll never end up like Maggie; although—who knows?—some day you may get the chance.

Harry Mathews

Praise for *Retelling*

The mystery of who butchered ethereally beautiful and pregnant Elsbeth is at the heart of Keller's elegant and spooky second novel (part of a trilogy, after *Jackpot*). Was it the traumatized and fragile narrator, Sally, whose friendship with the dead woman verged on the obsessive? Or was it Elsbeth's arrogant and demanding boyfriend, Drew, who resented Sally's relationship with her? Keller flirts with the answer as her novel slips back and forth through time to depict tantalizing glimpses of possible truths filtered through Sally's uncertain memories. The police, bent on extracting a confession from Sally, harangue her during increasingly abusive interrogation sessions that provide her a forum for creepily pondering her (questionable) innocence. This opaque yet beguiling novel showcases the work of a talented and original writer.

Publishers Weekly

Readers of Dostoyevsky's *Crime and Punishment* always know that Raskolnikov committed murder, but they often don't know whether Raskolnikov knows that he committed murder... In her new trilogy, Tsipi Keller is revealed as a superlative psychological novelist: "It was the end of the millennium, life rushed at me, the streets reeked of urine. Everybody talked but nobody listened. Men in suits shook hands as if important matters were at stake. It was all a game."

Joshua Cohen/The Forward

All of this gives the impression that Sally isn't someone you'd want to invite over for a nightcap—not without hiding the knives first. But *Retelling* is great at maintaining mind-bending suspense, and it never entirely rules out the possibility that its narrator is simply an odd case. The book questions its own sense of reality a few times too many, but the buildup is justified by the powerful final arc. In the end, Keller gives her narrator's eerie delusions free reign—an apt conclusion for this heartfelt and willfully perverse novel.

Michael Miller/TimeOut

What do you get when you mix a Rashomon narrative with a Hitchcockian detective esthetic? You get *Retelling*, by Tsipi Keller. Not only that, you get an us against them scenario that constricts tighter as it seemingly unfolds letting you know the universe has other plans beyond comprehension and to attempt understanding is to deal in frustration...In conclusion, we come away with a rich and tightly woven suspense story from Tsipi Keller, a master storyteller of the modern world, who assembles her palette of color and texture in the most exquisitely sensual ways... Not afraid to wear her influences on her sleeve, she does so humbly and without guile, as she offers her predecessors a grand and glorious complement by way of her deft display of mastery under their auspices.

C.B Smith/MadHatterReview

As in Keller's previous book, *Jackpot* (both novels are part of a planned trilogy), *Retelling* foregrounds a meek, solitary woman (the late Elsbeth once mocked Sally as "the little mouse, nibbling on books in the dark") who's bereft when her imperious pal disappears, leaving the beta-girl without a light source to illuminate her own half-formed personality... Capturing the waft and drift of her un-heroine's unstructured days, Keller has a keen eye for the territorial pissings and unspoken resentments of immature female friendships. *Retelling* is foremost a discomfiting novel of loneliness—perhaps we can all recognize some past or present version of ourselves in Sally, alone in the dark trying to piece together the shards of ugly memories.

Jessica Winter/The Village Voice

Praise for *Elsa*

Elsa is the third in Tsipi Keller's trilogy of psychological novels. The first two were *Jackpot* and *Retelling*, which trace the fortunes of women. Elsa calls to mind some of Richard Burgin's noir fiction. Both writers explore the world of nefarious, but initially engaging, operators who insinuate themselves into the lives of lonely strangers aiming to control or ruin them.... Much more than a tale about a smart woman who makes foolish choices, Elsa is a fast-paced, tightly crafted, suspenseful, psychological crime novel that sidles up to the reader, then pounces.

Lynn Levin/Cleaver Magazine

Elsa is a woman of thirty-nine: a tax lawyer who lives alone with her cat. She talks about men with her friends. She is a classic literary figure, a Madame Bovary in the twenty-first century. Tsipi Keller is more than aware of this, as Flaubert sticks his head in at one point: "The promise of love, faint as it is, does wonders for her. The promise of love, of romance, of beautiful sex. So what if women, to believe Flaubert, mistake their vaginas for their hearts? So what? Let them. Let her. What does Flaubert know about love? Let her mistake what part she chooses for her heart."

Evan Steuber/American Book Review

Praise for *The Prophet of Tenth Street*

Marcus Weiss is a middle-aged Jewish writer living in New York City, working on a novel called *The Reverse Turn of the Heart*, as well as a literary reference book— the Dictionary of the Human Gesture in Western Literature. His girlfriend Gina and best friend Oscar have nicknamed him "The Prophet of Tenth Street," "because he can't bear the idea that others... are not exactly like him." Marcus is neurotic like a Woody Allen character without the buoyant humor, obsessing over his literary pursuits, religion, women, love, and death. He produces his notebooks to quote Hitler and Maimonides for visitors ... Poet and novelist Keller (*Retelling*) handles this poignant tale with the deftness of a writer who has struggled alongside her characters.

Publishers Weekly

Tsipi Keller has taken us into a writer's very being.... This is a provocative story that stays with the reader.

Jewish Book World

It is beyond difficult to write fiction about a fiction-maker; not only do you have to get into the guy's hea⸍ you've got to create a plot in which something actu happens. Keller does both, and in a way that's unne⸍

-how does she know so much about what it means to be a man, trapped in his head, convinced he will find and reveal the essential truths of life?

Jesse Kornbluth

In elegant, pitch-perfect prose, Tsipi Keller explores what it means to be a writer in a post-Holocaust world. Her evocation of Marcus Weiss—at once tender and wise—lays bare the felt life of the novelist. Along the way, Keller pays honor to the human experience and to the artful language that gives us our measure.

Andrew Furman

Marcus Weiss preaches the love of literature in a wilderness where people don't read. Moreover, he is a writer. He is writing a book about himself writing, and about his lover and his friends, who wonder if they'll appear in his book. He exhorts them to read books that matter, that make us more human, that make the mind dance. And the marvelous thing is that the book he is writing, which is the one we are reading, is just such a book, because Marcus is generous, opinionated, foolish, and inspired, not merely a creature of words and paper. I'm sure he would add Tsipi Keller to his list of favorite authors if he knew her.

Joel Agee

Praise for *Nadja on Nadja*

Nadja's book title — but I see I'm speaking of Nadja as a person, not as a character in a novel; that's how seductive Keller is — suggests her acute self-awareness. "I have this idea about women in trouble of their own making," she tells her best friend. "Women who end badly because of their own gullibility and poor judgment. In fiction and in life."

Graduate students will note that "Nadja" is the title of a book by André Breton; it's one of the most significant works of French surrealism, posing the question "Who am I?" Keller is a gifted translator, mostly of Hebrew literature into English; she's won prestigious fellowships. You may confidently believe she was thinking about Breton's question and his title when she named her character. It is a testament to the high-wire act she has created that Keller has translated her erudition into prose in a way that doesn't show off anything but her talent.

Jesse Kornbluth/HeadButler.com

and

yes she

was

Tsipi Keller

Grateful acknowledgment is made to the following for copyrighted material:

Excerpt from Henry Miller's *The Wisdom of the Heart.* Copyright © 1960 Henry Miller. Reprinted by permission of New Directions Publishing Corp.

Excerpt from "Against the Evidence" from *Against the Evidence: Selected Poems 1934-1994.* Copyright © 1993 David Ignatow. Reprinted by permission of Wesleyan University Press.

Excerpt from "Berryman" from *Migration,* copyright © 2005 by W.S. Merwin, used by permission of Copper Canyon Press, www.coppercanyonpress.org.

May Swenson's "Women" from *New and Selected Things Taking Place* (Little Brown and Company). Copyright © 1978 by May Swenson. Reprinted by permission of The Literary Estate of May Swenson. All rights reserved.

Excerpt from Friedrich Reck's *Diary of a Man in Despair.* Translated from the German by Paul Rubens. Published in English by New York Review Books. Copyright © 1966 by Henry Goverts Verlag GmbH, Stuttgart. Translation copyright © 2000 by Paul Rubens.

Excerpt from "Tamer and Hawk" from COLLECTED POEMS by Thom Gunn. Copyright © 1994 by Thom Gunn. Reprinted by permission of Farrar, Straus and Giroux.

Unsolicited Press
Portland, Oregon
www.unsolicitedpress.com
orders@unsolicitedpress.com
619-354-8005

Cover Design: Kathryn Gerhardt
Editor: Chandler S. White; S.R. Stewart
ISBN: 978-1-950730-48-3
Library of Congress Control Number:2019952303

Writings contain HUMILITY, that is, self-knowledge.

—Alexander Kluge

I do not need to make phrases. I write to bring certain circumstances to light. Beware of literature. I must follow the pen, without looking for words.

—Jean-Paul Sartre, *Nausea*

A sad condition
To see us in, yet anybody
Will realize that he or she has made those same
    mistakes,
Memorized those same lists in the due course of the
    process
Being served on you now.

—John Ashbery, "A Wave"

and yes she was

mad at the time, she was married, her marriage had
taken her away from the city and planted her in a small
college town where her husband taught rich girls the
basic tenets of History and Culture. The girls had
arrived from all over the country with their horses—
the girls lodged in the dormitories, the horses in the
stables—and she, let's name her Annette, tried to
imagine the wealth and privilege that came with such
accoutrements.

Only in America, she thought, and yet she also
wondered how the purportedly spoiled girls managed
their busy daily schedules, but they did, they seemed to
thrive in the fresh air of intellectual and physical
pursuits, while Annette, not much older than the girls,
felt she had become something she never imagined was
possible, she became a staid housewife, or, to put a
finer spin on it, a staid faculty wife, living in a house
rather than an apartment, with plants and curtains and

I

pots and pans and china sets. It was nearly perfect but not quite, her soul, or something in her, suddenly made itself known, it began to agitate, and she, who used to be carefree and nonchalant, now felt, more often than not, disgruntled and old.

And yes, she did have a graduate degree in English Literature and she could, theoretically at least, teach composition, or give a writing workshop, but she couldn't see herself standing in front of a class, assuming the authoritative demeanor and mantle of scholarship, it would be a sham, she wasn't really qualified, she didn't think, but she did feel qualified to read books and possibly write and finish one if the stars above and perseverance on her part joined forces.

One morning, sitting in her sun-flooded kitchen—and yes, she had to admit, she loved to sit in her new kitchen, she loved the fact that she could sit in it, something she couldn't do in her New York City railroad apartment where the kitchen was basically a counter and a sink, right next to the old clawfoot tub shower she had a hard time climbing into, while her new kitchen was a real room, it was spacious, with high-ceilinged windows that faced the backyard where tree leaves fluttered in the breeze, waving effervescent hellos, and, when in the right state of mind, she believed they were waving at her.

And so that morning, sitting in her kitchen and plowing through nagging thoughts about her future and her marriage, she reached for the notebook where she wrote down emergency and other important telephone numbers, as well as her grocery shopping and To Do lists. She liked the notebook, it was her steady and efficient assistant, helping her to systemize and maintain order in her chores, prioritizing them by placing a number next to each. But she also resented the notebook because as she wrote the lists—only to be crossed out when done, only to begin a new one in the days to come—she couldn't help thinking that much of living one's life went into organizing one's life, which, at times, felt like an exercise in futility.

But that morning, with the notebook open before her, an image began to form in her mind, an image of herself sitting in the kitchen and writing a diary, no, two diaries, one she would title, Squabble Diary, and the other, Love Diary, or, more precisely, Sex Diary, in which she would record the times her husband deigned to touch her.

And then, just like that, she began, starting with the date, October 14, 1979, and, looking at the white page, unsure where and how to go from here, she focused on the date in the top left corner and then, a decision made, she added the hour—10am—and was soon on her way.

Here I am, at my kitchen table, starting a diary like a twelve year old, but a twelve year old who is already saddled. I'm hoping that the diary, at the very least, will help me to unburden myself. I know that even if I had someone to talk to, I'd be too embarrassed to share all that I need to share, or worse, once I start, who knows what else would pour out of me.

I feel I must create a space that's mine alone, a space where I can talk to myself and also describe in detail all squabbles with hubby, so that in the future I can go back in time and read and maybe understand, once and for all, when why and how they come about. Maybe there's a hidden logic, a frequency to be discerned, a deep-rooted misalignment and its inevitable aftermath.

Needed as well is a diary wherein to record our sexual encounters to later study the frequency in that department as well and delineate possible correlations. The Squabble Diary, no doubt, will be richer, more varied, and, alas, more frequent; were it otherwise, I wouldn't be sitting here, stewing in impotent acrimony and writing such drivel.

And it's not like we've been married forever, this is our fifth year as a couple, we got married two years ago, and before that we lived together for three. Except for the wedding bands adorning our fingers, not much has changed, our fights are as ugly and disturbing as they were before we got married. Apropos, my husband proposed to me on St. Patrick's Day, against the background din of a Blarney Stone Pub on Third Avenue, no doubt hoping to whitewash a fight we'd had the night before. And even though we'd already imbibed a few beers and felt very cool and pleased with ourselves, it was still a noisy Blarney Stone, not quite a romantic setting for marriage proposals. There was no going down on your knees, a rose in one hand, a ring in the other; rather, it was more in the vein of a suggestion made on the spur of the moment, a simple, and possibly desperate, possibly spontaneous "Hey, let's get married" from him, and a simple, and possibly timid, possibly confused "Okay" from me, and then the two of us smiling and laughing with a sense of having accomplished something, of having stepped over a hurdle, or a milestone.

Milestone or not, I don't feel "married" at all. I don't feel a deep-tissue/heart connection to him as I think I should, and I don't think he feels a connection to me. I think that for him marriage means stability, be it between two robots waking in the same bed every morning, eating at the same table, and signing the same Hallmark cards. No need and no time for idle talk, for amorous cuddling, for hanging out on the couch, side by side, doing nothing but breathing together mouth to mouth, exchanging sweet-saliva kisses.

As things stand, I can't even remember when we did it last, but I'm sure that at least two weeks have gone by and, except for a fleeting masturbation session he granted me a few days ago, there's been nothing at all. I'm not religious, but the Talmud says that sex is a married woman's right. Not only should a husband give his wife abundant sex, he should also make sure she is enjoying it. He should also be attentive to signs that his wife wants sex without her having to ask for it.

So, okay, my husband is not Jewish, he has other problems, but regardless, his strategy is to shirk all responsibility, telling me I should be more patient, more understanding, thereby cleverly shifting all sympathy/empathy duties on to me.

True, he is busy at the college, and he is also working on a book. After all, it's a new position for him, he's associate professor and he must prove himself and do research and publish if he is to get tenure. He is a dedicated teacher and, need I mention, a young generation of females depends on him, on his brilliance, hanging on every word that makes it to his lips as they dutifully take notes, and therefore, it so seems, I'm supposed to pleasure myself or find a fuck on the side.

Pfui, Annette, watch your language!

And if I sound bitter, I am, he's turned me into a bitter person, I'm too young to be/feel bitter, and "bitter" was never my thing. Still, I sometimes wish I were a different person, less "romantic" and more matter-of-fact practical, more mature, more deliberate, but I also know enough to know that I can't be someone I am not.

To the point: a squabble last night October 13. During the day my mood was kind of lukewarm, and then, in the afternoon, it veered toward lousy, if mildly so, not yet the acute and vicious kind, and by the time Monsieur arrived in the evening I was agitated, enveloped in morosity for the simple reason that my labors at stove and oven—Quiche Lorraine—resulted in a flop, but then, happily, my bad mood dissipated because we went out to eat, and he was nice, and then he went back to his office, and I sat down at my desk and wrote a few lines that could lead to something, or would point me in a certain direction, to an opening that would widen, and thanks to those few lines I was in an excellent mood and waited impatiently for him to come home so I could tell him right away that I did manage to write something (this past week I've written nothing, which, of course, doesn't help my mood), and I was also going to tell him that I found a solution to a story I'd told him about in the restaurant.

And so I sit at home and read, waiting for him to arrive, and then it's 11pm, 11:30pm, midnight, and I begin to simmer, and my desire to tell him anything evaporates and I decide not to tell him a thing, for what's the point of sharing with someone I hardly see. And, as I'm simmering, I find it hard to concentrate on the book I'm reading, and this makes me even more simmery, and, in a flash, I decide that since I can't connect with the words on the page, I might as well leave the house and go for a ride through the dark and empty streets of our sleepy town to clear my head of unhelpful thoughts, with the added bonus that when he finally gets here he won't find me waiting with nothing to show for myself but a rotten mood.

At 12:20am I quickly get dressed and run out of the house before he shows up and foils my plan. I'm thoughtful enough to leave him a short and cheerful note, saying I went out, see you later, and, like a thief, quickly get in the car and speed away.

I come back around 1:30am, shout a happy Hello to Monsieur and go into the bathroom to pee. Monsieur sits in the living room and watches TV (what's got into him all of a sudden, watching TV in the middle of the night). To make long short, my "brief" note didn't please him, he was worried, why didn't I explain in greater detail, and I say that it didn't occur to me that he would worry, after all, I did leave a note. I also promise (why?) that next time I will leave a longer note, and, aiming for more emphasis and clarity, I add (and this is the truth) that I didn't know where to and for how long I'd be gone and that's why the note was brief.

But, my explanation doesn't appease him, quite the contrary, as he goes on and on about the stupid note, and I, losing my patience, begin to agitate, but I'm still in a good mood thanks to my rebellious act, and I explain further and say that I was in a hurry and, frankly, was not going to leave a note at all, and here he goes ballistic and the fight is on. It ends after two hours of a hostile sit-down in the kitchen with wine and cigarettes, as I, all the while, remind myself that I'm trying to smoke less, but, on the other hand, when in crisis mode, one must not deny oneself, one is allowed, even invited, to indulge. Indeed, it's possible that the both of us create these dramas during which we can freely and darkly imbibe sorrow, tobacco, and alcohol alongside silent self-recriminations.

This morning, he's a new man, dripping love and sweetness, telling me that this week or next he'll take a day off and won't go to his office so that he and I can spend some time together. Hallelujah!

I forgot to mention that last night I also told him that from now on I want us to do as we please, he can come and go as he pleases, and I'll come and go as I please, and I think that this declaration of independence is what caused his sudden and, no doubt, temporary "reawakening" this morning. He probably got anxious about me disappearing in the middle of the night, and/or about the prospect that I might get busy with activities outside the home, in which case he'd lose the luxury of a little wife cooking and shopping and cleaning and sitting in an empty house waiting for him. In fact, the reason I fled last night was precisely because I didn't want to be here when he got home. I wanted him to know that I would not always be here, sitting and waiting. I wanted him to have a taste of what it feels like to sit and wait, day after day after night, having been transplanted to foreign soil in a friendless environment. So, that's it. Squabble number one to start, and to be continued.

And also to be mentioned is the fact that my period is due. According to the calendar it should have arrived today, or even last night, but it didn't. It's possible that because of my emotional distress and frustrations, my menses decided: This month I'm staying put!

I think that at my core I'm a feminist, not in the sense of movements and slogans, but a feminist the way most women are in the world, and always have been, natural feminists since time immemorial, not because of one theory or another but because of their life experience. Feminists in the sense of self-preservation, of wanting/seeking justice, of: Enough is enough. Some open their mouths and rebel (and often get killed), while others keep quiet but are consumed by a growing resentment within. A good example: my mother-in-law, who, at times, does let show a flicker of anger—no, rage—precisely now when her husband, getting on in years, is nicer to her, or so it seems to me, the outsider.

And what about me? Where am I in this mosaic of marriage and the pledge of everlasting love? Time will tell. Meantime, you, little book, are the place where I can talk to myself, where no one eavesdrops, and no one doubts or contradicts me. And: no more To Do lists. If I remember, I remember, and if I forget, I forget.

Saturday night. Monsieur had spent the day in his office, presumably working on his book; arrived here for dinner, served by his maid and lasting ninety minutes, then off he went to the college again, and then, at 11pm, he returned. For the duration of the night—ha! We are not in a state of war, but rather in what one might call détente. We're quiet, we don't speak. I'm writing in the kitchen, he sits in his chair in the living room, reading. When he came home for dinner, he announced, sorrowfully, that he is not happy. I think he expected to elicit a reaction from me, stormy or otherwise, but I stood my ground, saying nothing at all, for how do you respond to such a dead-end, deadening comment after standing in the kitchen, preparing his dinner. My silence meant: "If you have a problem, try to solve it. Don't blame me or come to me for answers," but I doubt he gets it.

I also think he doesn't understand how strongly and miserably and negatively I feel about this asexual life we're leading, that he is leading, and I, since we're attached, married, chained to one another, am also compelled to lead. I should have known. There were early signs, right from the start. The stories he told me. About a girlfriend who'd left him for a woman. About his father who'd caught him with a dirty magazine and threatened to cut off his thingy. About his fear of intercourse and disease. I thought that with me everything would be different, that love would triumph (how juvenile!), and now I'm stuck. I can't tell him that I need and want sex, because, as he informed me many times in the past, it would only put pressure on him (gevalt!), it would aggravate him, make him feel inadequate, and certainly would not bring about the desired erection. So, I keep my mouth shut.

Still, I don't understand how he doesn't get it. Or, maybe he does, but chooses to ignore it and say nothing, because, what is there to say when it is clear that the problem rests with him. But sometimes, à propos of nothing, he does suddenly announce that he has no sexual drive at the moment because his mind is on his work. And then, as any conscientious scholar, he introduces references from the past as proof that when he's busy at work, sex, necessarily, is pushed to a dusty, dark corner. And so, the days of my youth go by. I'll be thirty soon, a grownup, even if I don't feel I'm a grownup. I'm not even sure I know what grownup actually means.

Ah, well, no point dwelling on this, except to ask myself: why do I persist in this marriage? We're two beings who hurt one another. We can't help ourselves. We are who we are, stubborn and blind. I keep reminding myself that hope is pain. Or so says the Buddha. And I, I was raised on hope. And pain.

Like most people—says a small voice in my head.

Yes, but... There's always a but. Every language accommodates the need for, Yes, but.

I should mention that as a faculty wife I do have privileges attached, and I'm allowed to take as many courses as I like, gratis. I take a Life Drawing class, with live naked models, all females, alas, and also a Psychology class, given by Lester. Lester and his girlfriend Nell, both originally from New York, live in the next town and are our only friends here. Lester who told us that every time he enters the classroom he's overpowered by a strong and pervasive female odor, which got me wondering if it's my odor that's overpowering him.

We were staying over in their house that night, and later, when we all went to bed, I happened to glimpse Lester's bare and white ass. I was coming out of the guest bathroom, and Lester, naked, was walking down the hallway and into their bedroom, where Nell, presumably also naked, lay waiting, and it was such a pleasing and revelatory sighting that right there and then I forswore nightgowns, deciding that I, too, will sleep naked, and ever since that night I go naked to bed, and Monsieur, who loves pajamas and clings to them, doesn't understand what has happened to me, his little wife, why naked, he asks, and I say, I don't know, it's more comfy and soothing when I cuddle up with the duvet.

Reading Hermann Hesse's *Steppenwolf*, I came upon a passage that illumined something for me, and I've been sitting here, reading it, then gazing out the window a while, and then rereading it. This is not to say that my daily life is awash in contentment (ha!), but I do hear what Hesse is telling me. Like him, I do find myself sometimes in a kind of an unendurable contentment, a kind of passivity, and yes, an involuntary submissiveness. And I definitely hear the whisper of the days passing by on tiptoe. He says that there's much to be said for contentment, but after a while he is filled with hatred and nausea and must throw himself on the road of pleasure, or the road to pain. Yes, Herr Hesse. At times, even the road to pain is preferable.

Hello Squabble Diary. I'm back, and sooner than I thought. We fought again, and I was about to add "because of me." I don't know if this is indeed the case, or the simple fact that Monsieur has managed to bring me around to believing that all discords originate from me. A couple of days ago he confirmed his plan to take today (Friday) off, which he did, and so, earlier today, I asked him to do something for me (I don't remember now what it was, I may have asked him to plant the seedlings that have been waiting for three weeks on the counter) and he made a face and said it was his day off (incidentally, what about my day off? which, of course, didn't occur to me to ask). Then he said he'd do it. He also said he'd help me with the laundry. Great. And then? He disappears.

Gone to his office, I assume. Fine. I wasn't upset, even though he'd promised we'd spend the day together. I tried to reach him several times during the day, but no answer. So, he is not in his office but is hanging out somewhere, avoiding laundry, seedlings, and a nagging wife, a clichéd wife he's assiduously endeavored to create. Or, he is in the office, ignoring the phone. Meanwhile, I'm here, doing the work, cleaning, cooking, and for what?

When he finally came home, I couldn't help myself and complained that he wasn't here to help me

13

with the laundry and the seedlings, and so another night of sour hearts and sullen faces and a squabble entry in this notebook.

My beloved Stendhal speaks directly to me and sustains my spirit. Always. He, and other writers, too. I'll be quoting them now and then, but first Stendhal: "To write anything but the analysis of the human heart bores me."

And Anatole France is close behind: "A mind that is not uneasy irritates and bores me."

Hello Sex Diary. Finally, after a long hiatus, yesterday (Wednesday). Not great, but something. A crumb. For now, no additions to the Squabble Diary. Better this way.

Sex Diary. Yesterday, Sunday afternoon. No intercourse, but he went down on me. Good enough!

But, sitting here, pen in hand, it occurs to me that it is not exactly sex that I want. I want love and affection. A gesture, a touch, a word. I need to feel I am part of a togetherness that is vibrant and alive, rather than an entity that fills the slot of partner in the daily routine. Maybe it's true what they say about couplehood. At first it's romance and roses, and then real life kicks in and you're two people sharing a bed and insecurities.

And, to add a pertinent fact about other living creatures: life for a fly is precious. The life span of a fruit fly is about forty days, and the fly, I am sure, knows this, for the fly, like every living thing, has a built-in clock. I try to imagine what life is like when it spans only forty days, and the only answer: intense and purposeful. Indeed, flies, when they mate, cling to one another for about twenty minutes, quite longer than most humans devote to the act.

Had a comforting, idyllic dream about my mother. We're in the kitchen (mine? hers?), there are two pots on the stove, she has prepared two kinds of dishes for our dinner, and I say that I'll prepare yet another dish, and she is sweet and accepting, but she does say, "Are you sure we need another dish?" and I look again at the pots, still deliberating/deciding what I want to do. The dominant color in one pot is white, in the other, sort of pinkish, and both concoctions look like they have potatoes in them. I love potatoes, and I say, "No, of course not, this is fine, I'll just make a salad."

As I write, hot tears roll down my cheeks. There's so much regret between us. I do love and sometimes miss her, from afar, but when we're together I'm on the alert, waiting for her to say something I don't want to hear, and, when she does, I cut her short, and she is hurt and bewildered, not recognizing her sweet baby daughter, her firstborn. The thought comes that I mistreat my mother the way Monsieur mistreats me, but I soon reject it because it feels farfetched and superficial. My mother and I go back thirty years, and there's a lot of water under the bridge. Monsieur and I go back a few years and the ground under our feet is rocky and arid.

Squabble Diary, Saturday night. Well, hello to you, sir, I'm here again. And yes, I call you sir. I don't know why, but I can't picture you as a woman. I see you as an old, gentle man, someone who's been around and seen it all, someone who tolerates my handwritten— nearly illegible even to me—laments.

So, how did it go? Yesterday afternoon Monsieur and I went to a cocktail party, or that's what they call it around here. The invitees are established, law-abiding citizens, most of them professors. They have homes, cars, bank accounts, and some also have a child or two. But, as it turns out, I'm not the only outsider in this small and conservative town, there are a few gays and lesbians who have arrived from other parts to teach where Monsieur is teaching; discreet at their place of work, they let go on the weekends. What's interesting to me is that they chose to come here, but, as Lester says, a job is a job and tenure is tenure.

When we arrive, the party, it seems, has already reached its peak. All present are a bit tipsy, and the master of the house, Jewish and gay, is playing the piano, while the assembled guests are boisterously doing their best to sing along. Monsieur and I are somewhat taken aback, we did not expect pianos and singing. I spot a couch pushed against the wall and, a glass of white wine in hand, I make my way over, nodding here, nodding there, and sit down. Alone. Monsieur is talking to a couple of serious, older-looking professors, sporting trimmed beards. No mustaches.

Everyone is drinking, but because I have a cold and my nose is dripping and my eyes are tearing, I decide not to smoke and to drink only one glass of wine. I sit and slowly sip my wine and observe the guests. No one pesters me with idle chitchat because most of them don't know me, and those who do, know I have an accent, which means that one has to make an effort to understand what I'm saying. Lester and Nell were also invited but they politely declined, saying they were exhausted and needed quality time alone.

Laughing and shouting, the merry guests play all sorts of games, and even dance a little. The piano, meanwhile, has been abandoned, and a record is playing. Monsieur comes over and joins me on the couch, and now the both of us observe the scene. He informs me that he and I are the only hetero couple present. I don't know why he's telling me this, so I nod and say nothing. I know that Janice, one of the dancers, is married to Larry, but Larry, it seems, didn't make it to the party, or, he came and left early, leaving Janice behind to drink as much as she wants and act free and wild and single. She teaches science and has two PhD degrees, but when one is drunk, degrees do not interfere.

17

As I watch her, she sashays over to us and practically pulls Monsieur off the couch—she wants him to dance with her—and when he, after much protestation and attention-grabbing, finally rises, she insists on teaching him a certain move she wants him to perform: he is to spread his legs wide and hold her hands tight and she will glide under him, through and between his legs, to emerge triumphant on the other side. And since it takes her a while to verbalize exactly what she wants him to do, and since words are not readily available to her except "Between your legs!" "Between your legs!" everyone is laughing hysterically, including me.

And, right before this danse macabre episode, Monsieur tells me that one of the lesbians, tenured and in her late forties, came over to him earlier to tell him that she likes him, especially now that he has cut his hair and she can see his face, and that she wants the two of us, Monsieur and I, to come to a party she'll be giving soon. So, more invitations will be coming our way. People are discovering that we—fresh blood—are here, and our social circle is widening, thanks to Monsieur, of course.

We finally agree it's time to leave—most of the guests have already gone home, and the only people left are the next-door neighbors of the host and his lover. We say our goodbyes and leave, and as Monsieur starts the car, he asks: "How would you define manliness?" And since the subject is not paramount in my mind, and since definitions, by definition, elude me, I say: "Hmmm, I don't know. How would you define it?"

And here he explodes, saying that I don't answer his questions, that I answer a question with a question, and his attack is so absurd, I start to laugh, thinking he's joking, even though his tone doesn't suggest that he is, and we get into an argument that turns into a fight at home, and I, tired of talking, pick up a book and go to the bedroom to read, and he dashes to another room, in all likelihood to his desk, and I recall reading about a couple, both of them writers, who, after a long and satisfying fight, rush to their respective desks and diaries to report everything about the vileness of the other, pouring their dark hearts out on the page, instead of trying to make peace.

And—I'm thinking further—life with Monsieur is becoming more and more unbearable, not to say detrimental, it feels as though the only thing we're both good at and know how to do well is to get ourselves into an argument, and, looked at from all sides, this is not a healthy relationship.

I lie in bed and try to read, and Monsieur appears and begins to pace the room, wearing down the shiny wood floors, telling me he's upset because he's leaving for New York in the morning (he's promised John, his brother, to help him paint his new apartment), and he doesn't want to leave with the both of us in a bad mood.

I say that I understand, and we agree to forgive and forget, and then he says he wants to tell me why he asked me about virility. "Manliness," I correct him and instantly regret it, and he says, "It's the same thing," and I'm thinking, no, it's not the same thing, but I keep quiet and let him get things off his chest, and he says that at the party he felt that the lesbians in the room kept looking at him and he felt that they were thinking that here was a man—Monsieur—who could understand them and penetrate their unknowable depths (my wording).

I lie in bed, still holding the book in my hands, and I can't believe what I'm hearing. I'm thinking of telling him that he is not very manly when it comes to reading situations, least of all, reading women, and, as we both know, when it comes to sex there are knots and snags in his head he has yet to untangle, and when he goes down on me during sex it is only because a friend told him long ago that if a man goes down on a woman she is his forever, but, of course, I don't deliver myself of this short, custom-made monologue. Instead I say that I think he's in a confused state of mind because of the drinks he's had, and because he was surrounded by women who couldn't care less about sex with men and he saw them as a challenge to what he likes to call "manliness." In response he says that I'm wrong, that, on the contrary, he felt that he and they were in sync, and that he was at the center of attention, and he even sensed that a couple of them were pining for him because they're sexually frustrated and they would have liked to have a man like him in bed.

As I'm writing this, I'm amazed all over again that I actually had to listen to such gibberish. Still, I managed to keep my cool because I know how childish and self-centered/satisfied he sometimes is, especially when he drinks.

We go to sleep, and early this morning he wakes me up when I'm deep in a dream and want to remain in it, but he wakes me and again apologizes for last night. It's always the same scenario when he drinks too much, he becomes a wannabe philosopher—aggressive and argumentative and on the attack—and the next morning he apologizes, and I say, "All right, all right," just to end it.

So I say, "All right, all right," and he says that he decided not to stay in the city overnight, but come back tonight and set out again tomorrow morning. Not surprisingly, I don't like the idea, I don't want him around, and a couple of days alone is exactly what I need, but to him I say that it doesn't make sense to drive back and forth, and besides, I may need the car, so he should take the bus and stay the night, as planned.

He doesn't like it, he is hurt, but I really don't care. All I want is to be left in peace and go back to my dream, but then, when he leaves the bedroom, something—relief that he left the room?—breaks open in me and I begin to cry, it is sad, sad, sad, or I am sad, sad, sad, and bewildered, and torn, seeing no end/resolution to our problems. Then he comes back into the room (I'm done crying by then, so he doesn't know I've been shedding tears), and again he apologizes, and again he inflames my nerves, and I tell him to leave me alone and let me sleep, and again he leaves, and again I cry, out of exasperation, anger, despair, I want PEACE, I want him out and gone, and again he comes into the room, and so back and forth, until he finally leaves for the city, and I'm shedding my last tears as I gradually calm down and sleep, like a teenager, until one in the afternoon, at which time I get myself out of bed and make breakfast.

Before that, around noon, I think, he calls from New York and I tell him that I'm still sleeping and

21

that I'll call him when I get up. And so, after breakfast, I call him, and again he says he'll come back in the evening, and this time I say I prefer that he remain in the city and that I need to be alone. There's a long pause, but then he says okay, and we hang up.

Later, I went grocery shopping, and then drove around a bit, listening to classical music and lulling in my head, gradually coming back to myself and feeling normal again. I read all afternoon/evening, and then, like a convalescent, gobbled down a large and delicious dinner, I even baked bread, and for the first time in a long time I prepared a meal for myself only(!), a juicy cheese and bacon omelet, a spinach and tomato salad, seasoned with chopped garlic, black pepper, olive oil, and squeezed lemon juice, and now, sitting here, I feel content. He called about half an hour ago and I told him I'm feeling better, and he said he was going to the movies with John, and I said, "Have a good time."

And that's the story. And my cold is gone, too, so, for now, all's well, except that it occurs to me that his obsession with "manliness" and lesbians may have to do with his former girlfriend who left him for a woman. I could, of course, bring it up during an argument, he certainly would if there were an equivalent occurrence in my past, but what's the point. The more important question: why do I remain in this marriage? My mother always advised: "If you marry, marry someone you can divorce," namely, someone who wouldn't give me a hard time, and Monsieur, I know, will be easy to divorce, he won't make scenes and he won't object. For all I know, he may be contemplating the same eventualities, but is waiting for me to take the initiative and point the way. Mystery! It

22

is not God's ways that are a mystery, but people's brains.

And talking of brains: it is good old Tolstoy and his wife Sophia who rushed to their desks and wrote in their diaries, inviting posterity to be the judge.

It's been a while since I last wrote—a lot has happened—but nothing to complain about. Monsieur and I, for the most part, are getting along swimmingly, and therefore when I read what I've written above, it all seems far and removed. Indeed, a mystery. My own brain is a mystery to me. It's as if I've been underwater for a long time and have suddenly emerged, equipped with a new personality and patience. We'll see how long it lasts. One thing is certain: we won't stay here beyond this year. As soon as the school year is over, and a few other technicalities are taken care of, we're out of here.

It all started when one of Monsieur's colleagues— Thomas, who was part of the committee that interviewed him, and who was the one who actually hired him—told Monsieur that he was not happy with Monsieur's attitude, blah blah, blah. He said that Monsieur didn't devote himself enough to the college and the students—absurd!—and that he had to try harder. Monsieur said nothing, and came to his dear wife and told her and we both agreed that Thomas was jealous of Monsieur's success with the students, and we decided on the spot that we'd had enough of this

23

picture-perfect sleepy town and that it was time to go back to the city—home!

And so, as said, we've been getting along fine. Now and then, a sudden spark threatens to ignite and turn into a fight, but it is soon extinguished and we continue peaceably as before, as if this is our natural and normal state, and for this, at least in part, we must thank Thomas, who galvanized both of us to fight the common provincial enemy. Also true is the occasional, and thankfully brief, mental flash that says that we're both trying to hold it together until we're done packing and moving and are settled in New York.

Lester—also a New Yorker and now stuck here, wishing he could extricate himself from the Tenure Lure, as he calls it—was so upset to hear this Thomas story, that he, too, said that Monsieur shouldn't allow Thomas to talk to him the way he did, and that if we can afford it, we should say goodbye to this golf/ghost town, even though he doesn't want to lose us, the only sane couple around—well, comparatively speaking, and Lester is a psychologist. And, in a few months, we will. Goodbye provincial living, goodbye big house and spacious sunny kitchen (the only thing I'll miss), goodbye countryside and winding roads and golf carts and having to get in a car to buy a bagel. Goodbye to all that, and Hello Big City—crowded, noisy, smoky, smelly, and, best of all, alive, restless, screwy, goofy.

Monsieur bought me a present, a fountain pen, and I'm now writing with it, watching the letters as they form on the page in vibrant blue ink. Last night I finished a new draft of my story "Fat Chance" about a housewife who sits on her couch one night, kissing an orange. She didn't mean to kiss it. It happened around 11pm, her husband, heavy with wine, had gone to bed around nine, and she gets an orange from the fridge and goes back to the TV in the living room, and, as she sits down on the couch, preparing to peel the orange, she becomes aware of vague sensations coursing through her, and instead of peeling the orange she begins to fondle it, admiring its oval shape, its rough texture, and then, suddenly inspired, she brings the orange to her lips and begins to kiss it, at first the lips are doing the kissing, but then, what began as a kind of experiment, escalates to full romance, and her tongue gets involved, as well as her horny imagination, and she licks and kisses and even gives little bites of passion, and as she observes herself in her mind, half mocking, half enchanted, she finally bites into the skin and begins to peel her lover and then she eats it.

This woman is not a stranger to me. She could have been me a few short weeks ago. Now, as said, Monsieur and I are like two doves, looking forward to the promise of freedom when we'll be leaving this prison. Sex is still rare, but, at least, we're affectionate with one another, as every day brings us nearer the time when we'll be back in our natural habitat. It's also possible that we've entered a new phase in our relationship—time, as they say, will tell. For now, it's good.

I don't know whether or not there's a connection between my birthday (two weeks ago) and the general sense of futility/despair I've been carrying ever since I turned thirty. Suddenly I feel there's no time, suddenly I feel hurried, that I must finish the new story I'm working on, or at least devote more time to work, a feeling of urgency, new to me, feelings of guilt and regret for not doing more, for not working harder, more diligently. And, à propos, Monsieur told me yesterday that Lester had asked him if I'm okay. He said that I seem unhappy to him, sad and restless, and then he went on to speculate that it's because I'm not involved with life here, living in a small town that holds no interest for me. How does Lester know all this?

As Monsieur was telling me this, good-humoredly, adding that he now understands how difficult it must be for me to live here, that I have no one to talk to, something began to churn in me and, before I knew it, I began to cry. Monsieur was alarmed, fearing God knows what, but the fact is that I was crying because *I* became alarmed. I had no idea that others see me as a doleful person who's walking around depressed. I began to cry because if people can see on my face that I'm not well, it means that I'm really in a bad state. This conversation took place in Monsieur's office, a few minutes before I had to go to Lester's class and Monsieur to his class.

I got hold of myself, washed my face, smoked a cigarette, and went to class. After the lecture about Freud and sexual fantasies (titillating for the giggly young girls, and Lester, indulging them, gives a little smile and waits for them to calm down), Lester and I went up to his office, as we always do after class, to smoke and chat. Then, in passing, he mentions that he spoke to Monsieur about me because I seemed unhappy to him and that, if I'm interested, he can introduce me to a writers' group that meets not far from where he lives. I said I wasn't sure I was ready to join a group. My major problem, I explained, was discipline, and a feeling that I'm wasting time and not doing what I should be doing, and if I seemed sad and unhappy sometimes it was only because I was unhappy with myself for not sitting down and concentrating on work.

As I was speaking the words, a strange sensation spread in my head, a warmth that split my consciousness in two, one half speaking the words, the other, watching, reminding me that I was not telling Lester the exact naked truth, that I was skirting around the real reason why I look so sad and unhappy, and I considered, and rejected, the idea to tell him more, to tell him about Monsieur and I, tell him that I sometimes feel that I live with someone who is not there, tell him, tell him about a sexless marriage, but I couldn't, if only because I knew, sensed, that it would be unfair to burden him with such private and intimate details, details that, moreover, might suggest to him that I'm in need of a lover, and that this sudden confession is actually a "hint," or worse, an invitation.

I told him that I have the first draft of a novel I started a couple of years ago in New York, but now, in this new place, I can't get myself to start the second draft and do the "tedious" but necessary work, i.e., revise. I also said that it's not just the new place, it's me as well because I feel that I've done the real work, writing the novel, but I lack the necessary patience and focus to go through the "labor" of rereading and revising and rereading and revising.

But, again, as I was speaking the truth about my frustration with the novel, I still knew I was not saying what I really wanted and should have said, namely, to tell him about the "me" he knows nothing about, the "me" who's also new to me, a "me" who's in a sterile relationship and who therefore can't discipline herself, a "me" who can't accomplish anything, a "me" who is confused and who feels lost, a "me" who's looking for a way out but doesn't know which way to turn, and, once again, I couldn't/wouldn't confide in him and tell him what I really feel.

He then asked me what I do instead of working, and I said I find excuses, I need to do this or that, and often the excuse is that I feel like reading, and I end up reading and not writing. Once I'm done with my chores, I said, I'm with a book, sometimes from morning to evening, and as soon as I finish one, I begin another, and as soon as I begin another, I want to stay with it, which is yet another excuse/escape.

At first Lester suggested that maybe this is what I need to do now, to read, but then he gave me an idea that I thought/hoped might work. He said that when I think about writing but don't feel like writing, instead of grabbing a book I should reach for pen and paper and begin to write whatever comes to my head, write what I feel, write about my frustrations, write about guilt, anger, silence the critic in me and write. We agreed that when I know I have time to write but can't make myself sit down, I must reach for a pen and sit down and write.

Lester also advised to write in one particular place, preferably a place where I do nothing else, and that's where I am right now, at my desk in our work-library room. I've been here a few hours already, and, having worked on my baby-novel—baby in the sense of still growing and developing—I now come to you, little book, to tell you the good news of a morning well spent. I'm still sitting at my desk, even though I'm cold and it's more comfortable in the kitchen where it's warm and where the radio is and coffee and the fridge. But it's precisely because of these comfort distractions in the kitchen that Lester advised to sit elsewhere, and that's what I'm doing and, so far, it's working.

I'm also thinking that I should start writing a real diary, not the diary of a silly girl, but a more serious diary, talk about real things, about what's happening in the world, my impressions and feelings about events in the world, rather than about me and Monsieur.

Right now I feel great, actually happy, and what I don't understand is why it is so difficult for me to sit down and work if I know that when I do sit down and work a few hours at a stretch, I'm filled with gratitude and my heart is full. If I know that the mere fact of sitting down and working puts me in the right frame of mind and gets me thinking and engaged, why is it so hard to sit down and be with and in my brain?

And now it's time to stop and go to the kitchen and put delicious lunch food in my mouth and chew it. I hope to come back here later. With a sweater!

The Kabbala equates thoughts with angels. The Kabbala says that even the most mundane thought denotes that an angel is present, which may be true, but at times of conflict, the angels that visit my brain/mind, twirl and circle like dervishes and, for the most part, do not enlighten and are not benevolent. I ask myself what kind of brain do I have—is it defective? What kind of brain would torment its "mistress" like this? It's possible that my brain, formerly a reliable ally and supporter of my whims, doesn't like the person I've become, a whiner and a malcontent, and therefore it retaliates against me, hoping to shake me up and lead me back to the person I once was.

And so, here I am again, doing what Lester suggested: sit down and write even if/when I don't feel like it. But, in fact, I did feel like it, and have been feeling like it and working steadily day after day, but then, last night, and earlier tonight, had a squabble with Monsieur, not a verbal, face-to-face confrontation with him, but a mute one, in my own head, and this dramatic dialogue in which I played both parts, took the wind out of my optimistic white sails, and I now sit here, drained and exhausted and spiritless and hoping to revive myself.

To summarize: I've been working well for over a week, and yesterday I took a day off without any feelings of guilt, at least not consciously. Yesterday was also the first evening in a while that Monsieur was home early, we ate and talked and watched TV, and then Monsieur said he was going to bed and asked that I wake him in an hour. I read, and then woke him, but he didn't feel like getting up, so he continued to sleep, and I continued to read. Nothing new here, it's become a kind of a new routine in this house, the house that contains us, our "relationship": he goes to bed after dinner, asks me to rouse him, while we both know that he won't rise and will sleep till morning, and still I, like an idiot, go to the bedroom to wake him, he rolls over and mumbles, and this is it for the night. And the same scene, in every detail, repeated itself tonight.

Something is definitely wrong (again, nothing new here), our "union," or whatever it is, is not working. And I'm sick and tired of myself, of having allowed myself to be inducted into this sentry position. I'm sick and tired of writing about it, but it's on my mind, it's like a disease, and it eats at me. Something is wrong and it could be that, like he often says, I am to blame. I wonder if I'm normal, if I behave like a "normal" wife, if such a creature exists. I'm also thinking that at this very moment there are many other women who sit alone, listening to their snoring husbands, and having the same exact thoughts as me.

At any rate, if I am to blame, so be it, I am to blame, but this doesn't get me/us anywhere. It's true that I'm always, or nearly always, angry with him (no sex?)—he annoys and irritates me. He says that I don't "see" him. I'm not sure it's true, I think I see him only too well, maybe not the way he wants me to see him, but I see *him*.

But, let's assume that I don't see him, does he see me? Why does he need Lester, a stranger, to tell him that I'm unhappy? And why does he always accuse me of something? Is this his way of camouflaging his own shortcomings? Defense as offense? I'm irritable, does he not see that? Does he ask himself why? He probably knows why. And I'm not saying I'm perfect. I'm even thinking that it is not just him, it is also my own doubts and struggles—mostly having to do with the book—that make me anxious and irritable. Not to mention my doubts and anxieties about myself, my personality, doubts that, I often feel, he is only too happy to prod at with a stick.

And so I must conclude that it's everything together, and it weighs me down. His harangues remind me of my first boyfriend, my first lover, who once gave me LSD and I swallowed it, knowing nothing about the drug, or even that it was a drug, and, during the trip, he kept urging me "Come to my wave! Come to my wave!" which, at first, bewildered me, but as he kept repeating it, pushing his face in my face, his eyes flaming like torches, the thought came that if I went to his wave I'd be his forever, and this terrified me.

Why don't I say goodbye and leave? Am I a masochist? I don't think I am. Maybe, indeed, we're both waiting until we're resettled in New York. The good thing: I'll now try to go back to the novel and see what happens. Monsieur is asleep, the street is asleep, and the house, nice and quiet, is all mine, as well as the desk and the window, and the peaceful stillness of the trees outside, and the street lamp, shedding its soft light just for me.

A few months before she died, Clarice Lispector said in an interview that adults are sad and solitary. One may add: sad and solitary and sorry. Sorry in all senses of the word, a sorry sight, sorry for their lives, sorry for others, sorry sorry sorry. And I am an adult now, I think, at least number-wise if not mental-wise, adult and no adultery, yes, no adultery, and the same problem again, as was to be expected, things change in the world, but people, relationships, if fundamentally not a good match, things won't change, a bad match is a bad match and Monsieur and I are a bad match. Et voilà! Simple and clear and simply stated. No other/better way to express it.

And yet, we stick together. More downs than ups, and yet we stick together. A couple in the world. Also true is the fact that we both behave like children, we get mad at eacher (each other) for childish reasons, and in childish ways. I often berate myself and make resolutions, hoping to become a better, more patient person, and it may work for a spell, but then he does or says something, and I respond, and another fight erupts.

Do all married couples fall into a routine of repeated abuse and complaints followed by rote apologies? Not all, but certainly a great many. For most people, basic behavior patterns don't really change. We change physically, the mind accumulates knowledge, but we don't learn from mistakes. And emotionally, do we grow emotionally? We learn to hide our feelings.

Had a strange dream last night, strange in the sense that it was totally different from any dream I'd ever dreamt. I'm with my family—my mother, father, sister, cousins—and a few other people, relatives and also neighbors and strangers, there's a group of us and we're all in a forest, hiding among the trees, terrified. It is nighttime, and the Nazis are after us, they're closing in, we're determined to fight back but we have only one knife between us. Then the Nazis spot us, and one of them shouts (in English?): "Don't kill them!" And we know why: we are prisoners who escaped from a concentration camp, and he wants to use us as a warning to others in the camp to demonstrate what fate awaits those who attempt to escape. And here I woke up, shaken, and am still brooding over it.

The Nazis, I'm thinking, must have appeared in my dreams before, dreams that remained properly and deeply buried, never to surface; interesting that this one finally did. The Nazis are part of my history, my parent's history, my parents who survived the camps and met after the war. My father is eight years older than my mother, and, when they married, she was a twenty-nine-year-old virgin, or so my father claims; my mother, on the other hand, insists that she was not a virgin. She was marrying a widower, of sorts, since my father's first wife and their five babies had perished in the camps. A family my father told me about when I turned twelve.

It was the first and last time I saw my father cry, and I remember the shock of it, and also that I was puzzling over the fact that I could have had another mother, an idea that strangely enchanted me. I don't remember if I puzzled over it right then and there, or later, when I'd think about what he'd told me, and the image of this mysterious ethereal mother grew in my mind.

I don't think I knew what to make of the children, my brothers and sisters. I couldn't fathom or conjure up an image or a face, I couldn't connect them to me, I didn't know what or how I should feel. Years later my mother told me that the five children my father lost were not babies. The oldest was a girl of fifteen, the youngest, a boy of three, all of them destroyed in Auschwitz in 1944. Had to leave you for a moment as tears started flowing. Went to the bathroom and washed my face, then out to the front steps where I sat with coffee and cigarette and watched the sparrows hop from here to there, pecking the ground.

One more vivid image: my father and I are sitting in the living room, my father on the couch, and I in the armchair facing him. It is just the two of us, so it must be Friday night, late, everyone has gone to bed already, and, as he does every Friday night, he tells me stories about famous rabbis, like Maimonides and the Baal Shem Tov. And then, without warning, he suddenly disappears right before my eyes, furiously rubbing his palms together for what seems like a long time, a strange, faraway look in his deep brown eyes. First spitting into his palms, and then rubbing, rubbing until he reemerges, and we continue to talk.

I never asked him what he was doing, or why. On some level, I must have sensed that it was a difficult, private moment, and that I must not interrupt. This image comes back to me now and then, and I conclude that he was reliving the indignities he'd witnessed and suffered in the camps, as well as the destruction of his family, not only of his wife and kids, but the entire clan of his large orthodox family, and the close-knit community it was part of.

Haven't been here a while—apologies! But have been working on Book, working quite well on second draft, Monsieur and I are getting along, or, more precisely, we're both busy with our projects and let each other be. Maybe this is what marriage is about, leaving the other alone. Maybe the knowledge that the other is around is enough, but I want more, I want exuberance, I want to shout, I want a big, shared life with someone I love and who loves me, with many friends around, and dinners, and talking and laughing. I feel that I'm wasting my days here, with Monsieur, that I don't live my life as I would like to live it, and, worst of all, I'm tired of complaining to myself about myself. And it's cold and gray, I miss the sun, I want to sit in a park in the sun, or sit at a small round table in a nice sidewalk café and watch the people go by, but this is not the city, this is a small provincial town, not even a town, but a village, it's all homes, cars, and shopping centers in the middle of nowhere, the shopping center is the "there" and the only "café" I get to sit in once a week is really not a café at all, not even a cafeteria, it's a plastic counter in the all-plastic Kmart. I sit there and drink my tepid coffee and smoke a cigarette, while my laundry is spinning in the Laundromat next door.

The other day, as I was sitting there, waiting for my laundry and trying to read, I suddenly noticed a black man sitting a few stools away from me. He was an older man, maybe in his late fifties, and I looked and looked at him with what I can only describe as joy fused with philanthropy, in the original/literal sense of philanthropy. There aren't many blacks here, or practically none at all, and I was so glad to see him, I wanted to go up to him and whisper that he and I stand out among the people here, the people here, did I say, are all white and pale and oftentimes overweight, clad in haphazard synthetic pants and shirts, and when I sit at the counter and watch them, I idly ask myself if they, too, are waiting for their laundry, or are resting from shopping.

No doubt, the mood I carry with me colors everything. Even Lester's class no longer interests me, and the same is true of the drawing class. I don't remember ever such a period of despondency in my life, and all I can do is blame it all on Monsieur who brought me here and turned me into a recluse. I was never such a complainer, a whiner—and these conditions, too, I believe, I contracted from him.

Seeking a way out, I remind myself that this is not the end of the road, and that my sentence here will not last forever, I'll be leaving this place before long and then life, hopefully, will begin again.

Another thought offers itself and lingers, suggesting that it's not only Monsieur but also mysterious forces that are operating in/on me, and these forces are the cause of the inexplicable mood swings, of the sudden low spirits. There's no reason for me to feel in the dumps, nothing "bad"—nothing concrete—I can point to, just the usual day in and day out, and the usual need for human contact, affection, so Annette, better stop whining and do something— work! Work brings you closer to yourself.

I'm waiting for the day when I feel that this notebook has served its purpose and I can put it aside. I'm thinking that such a move may signal that something has changed in me and that I've "matured." At times I feel that this notebook is only a means to waste time, allowing the illusion of serious honest writing from the heart, which it is, for the most part, but it is also an outlet for discontent and self-pity. And even if I change my mind about this judgment tomorrow and want to take it all back, it's all right, too, because it is only me and me sitting here and no harm done.

And here is my good comforting companion these past few days, Henry Miller in *The Wisdom of the Heart*: "Our amusements are catered for by mechanized methods, for we cannot amuse ourselves … and it is to live in this disordered world that we bring up our children so expensively. The system is threatened with disaster, but we have no thought but to hold it up, while we clamor for peace in which to enjoy it. Because we live in it, it seems to be as sacred as ourselves."

Stretched the last yawn out of my body, and now here to report that work on the novel is slow but advancing reasonably well—at least that. Monsieur is away in New York for a job interview, and I have the house to myself. He wanted me to join him, but I said I didn't want to go, that I wanted to work, and he said that he doesn't understand why I can't work in the city, or leave my desk for two days, and I said that I can't, and

I stayed behind. More and more I feel I want, need, to be alone, this is quite a new feeling, and I welcome it, a new person is being born. More serious, more subdued, more dedicated to something, in this case, a book. At the same time, the "cold front" with Monsieur, and the mere fact that I sit alone and think, invites me to be quiet with myself and look back at the person I was and the person I think I am now.

I used to tell people and myself that life is a gift, that we should accept what is given and not expect or demand too much, but now such wise words no longer work for me, I can't help wanting, wanting, and wanting more, not because I'm greedy, but because I feel trapped, starved, unloved—in short, unhappy, and I'd rather be unhappy alone than unhappy with someone. Sometimes I ask myself why I remain in this marriage, or, do I want to remain in this marriage, and there's nothing there, no ready answer, only a blank, as if I have become a blank, unable to tackle the issue and push for a clear answer, for a clear and definite decision. But, I'm not alone in this. Millions of people, men and women, find themselves at a similar impasse, and poets have described it, like Mark Strand in his short poem "Coming to This." Here's the second stanza:

And now we are here.
The dinner is ready and we cannot eat.
The meat sits in the white lake of its dish.
The wine waits.

I know I've said it before but will say it again. I need more fun in my life, I need pleasure once in a while. I need to lose myself with another receptive soul. I need a warm smile, a laugh, and a few good words. This is not to say I get no pleasure at all, I do, when I work well (today not so well) and suddenly something happens, on the page and in my brain, and my entire being is pleasured. I'm not phrasing it right, but today my brain is not cooperating, so it'll have to do.

Rembrandt drew and painted his self-portrait many many times (ninety?), creating a sort of a visual autobiography, documenting the effects of time on his face, on his state of mind, in the sense that a state of mind is reflected in your face: self-portraits as a means to examine yourself, and, in that sense, it is a visual diary because a diary is also a self-portrait that evolves over the years, and I mean a real diary, not the kind I've been writing here, namely, a diary that, so far, is mostly about marital froideur, and complaints about no sex/dialogue. And so, enough with all that, it's time to grow up and look around as well, see others, talk with others, develop, and become a real person.

A lot of work yet to be done. I'm still young, but it doesn't mean that time is on my side, time is on nobody's side. Indeed, there's a new sense of urgency in my brain, my bones, urging me to work and to not waste time. It used to be that I never gave Time a thought, or, if I had any such thoughts, it was more likely to be, If not today then tomorrow, and now it's all about today, possibly because I've crossed the threshold of thirty. Who knows. Slowly but surely, I'm growing up. Maybe. Growing in years, certainly.

Also, have decided that I need to change the music I listen to all day, and switched from classical to rock that instantly makes me move and sway. This is what I feel I need, an uplift and total release, letting go, it's been a great while since I got drunk, not drunk-drunk, but party-happy drunk. I've become too limited, too controlled, too responsible, too goal-minded, too focused on "chores" and "things to do"—a real housewife who cleans and cooks and watches her work amount to nothing, for again she rises and cooks and bakes and cleans—while also trying to keep a functioning brain and do real work far away from the kitchen, working at her desk, which is good, but!

And, almost forgot to mention what I came to write here in the first place, talking about Rembrandt. He was a pauper when he died and was buried as such in a grave owned by the church. Twenty years later, as was customary with the poor, his remains were destroyed. This is humanity in a nutshell.

It's time to break loose, physically and mentally, clear my head of books, of thoughts, ambitions, plans, and dreams of a different, maybe impossible, exciting future, and instead of dreaming, take action. Even as soon as tonight, after I'm done here, at my desk. I don't need Monsieur or anyone for this, not to mention that Monsieur would never join me in this kind of orgiastic behavior, and so, I'll do it all on my own, turn up the volume and drink and dance and, if I feel like it, shout!

Later. 2am. Dancing my head off, my spirits soaring with Aretha Franklin and Michael Jackson. I'm in seventh heaven, I need nothing but music, loud music, and occasional breaks with wine and cigarette on the stoop, watching the night, watching the smoke leave my mouth against the dark sky and the soft light of the street lamp. Life is good and simple! Monsieur called at 11pm or so—he's in the city for another job interview, says it went well—good! I told him I'm going to bed, we hung up, and then the party began.

Had a productive day at my desk, and now here to talk more about pleasure, the pleasure to be got from work, and if the term pleasure is not exact, then a deep, profound, all-enveloping peace is. You've done your work, and then a peaceful contentment, a gift, and a feeling that you've reached a new plateau. It won't last, but for the time being, you're in your own private peaceful universe, you're immersed in it, nothing else exists, nothing else matters. In a strange way, you're empty of thought, you simply exist in peace.

And here's the second stanza from Thom Gunn's "Tamer and Hawk," I read it and reread it, and my heart soars with the lines as I try to imagine what it would feel like if sometime in the future I would have someone who would inspire such lines in me. But, right now, this minute, it is not absolutely necessary, or urgent:

Even in flight above
I am no longer free:
You seeled me with your love,
I am blind to other birds—
The habit of your words
Has hooded me.

Saturday. A black day. Nothing seems to work for me,
my brain is everywhere and nowhere, I'm in New York
with Monsieur, we've been here since Thursday
afternoon, and are finally going home tomorrow. We
looked at a few apartments we didn't like, we're staying
at his brother's, it's small and cramped and dark and
dusty, I can't wait to be back home, home in the sense
of being alone, at my desk, and with no one around.

This is strange because I like John. Unlike
Monsieur, John is fun, and I thought I'd be able to
work here, if not in the apartment then in a café, and I
am in a café right now, a couple of blocks from John's.
I sat inside for a while and managed to work for about
half an hour, and now, brain empty, I sit on a bench
they have on the sidewalk, it's a bit chilly, but okay,
yesterday was actually nice, the weather was pleasant, I
walked around town, went into Benetton's and bought
a little sweater on sale, then met with Lucy and Jamie
downtown (John lives uptown) and we jumped for joy
and kissed and hugged and then we went into St.
Marks Bookshop and browsed among the tall and
crowded shelves. I came out with Mary Oliver's
Twelve Moons, and then we sat in a café and talked, it
was so good to see them, to be with them, to talk to

people other than Monsieur. But, I haven't been able to sleep these past two nights, I toss and turn as if in a dream-daze, and I groan and moan, begging in vain to fall into a deep and restful sleep. Still, I sit here and urge and plead with myself to be patient and to please not worry about having "wasted" a couple of days.

But why am I sad? After all, I'm in New York, yes, in New York, but we don't have a home here, I feel like a stranger, a visitor, but not a happy visitor, everything is hanging, our future, and looking for a place to live, and so on. This is so unlike me, walking around gloomy, when I want so much to walk around smiling and in high spirits, anything to lift myself up beyond petty worries and uncertainties. I tell myself that this is a transition period, but a voice in my head tells me that it is this life in two—marriage—that weighs me down. Every little thing has to be discussed and agreed upon, you can't just go ahead and decide on something on your own.

And now I'm back on the bench with a glass of wine, rather than another coffee, and I smoke a cigarette. Soon, I'll go upstairs and join them, we'll go out to dinner, or Monsieur will cook.

On a balcony across the street, a man is yelling at his dog: "Bad dog," and then, again: "Bad! Bad!" He grabs the small black dog that has been cowering at his feet and carries it inside, where he can still be heard shouting: "Sit! Sit!" Presently, he reappears on the balcony, bending down to the floor, and I gather that he's cleaning after the dog. When he's done cleaning he walks back inside, and it's quiet, no more shouting at "bad dog," and I'm thinking that there will come a day when men like him could place an order and own a pre-trained, genetically modified dog that will never have an "accident" and will only poo, pee, and bark on command, a personalized, custom-made dog that would satisfy the whims of any fastidious dog-lover.

I sip my wine and smoke my cigarette, spirits somewhat better, hoping the wine I'm drinking, and the wine I'll have later with dinner, will help me fall asleep tonight, and now, I suddenly realize, the dog and the man are back on the balcony, and the man, again, orders the dog around, but the dog, it seems, has had enough and he barks at his master, "Bad man!"— which, of course, is not the best idea when dealing with masters of any stripe. The master raises his hand and teaches the dog a lesson, striking it on its back, and the dog runs to the corner and wails, and the master barks "Bad dog!" and grabs the dog and goes back inside. Unbelievable! Why would such a creature even want a dog? So he'd have someone to yell at?

Tomorrow we go home, and Monday I'll begin to type a whole new (last?) draft, incorporating the revisions I worked on, and making final (scary thought) decisions, learning, step by minute step, that every choice leads to the next, as your brain becomes more adept, more attuned to what you're after.

.

Here again, after three difficult weeks, nightly nightmares about "Cinderella in New York" (provisional title), words and images crowd my brain, one moment encouraging, the next, discouraging, and I'm tossed between them, agitated and bewildered.

Absolute torture, and no resolution in sight. And so I come to you, my little diary, because, as you know, we forget the things we have no one to tell them to, and if I don't tell it to you, it'll be lost. This may sound a little dramatic, but it's true, this is what I feel right now.

Today again I woke up with a heavy heart, a feeling of desolation, like I don't belong here, I belong nowhere, and I know myself enough to know that I don't really want to "belong," so why is this an issue. And yet, this general feeling of emptiness, of uncertainty and futility, is unsettling. I feel I don't belong among people, and, except for rare moments, I feel that what interests them (movies and shopping) doesn't interest me. I can tolerate chitchat, and sometimes even enjoy it, but I need/want something deeper, something to engage the brain, the spirit, I want the kind of conversation that brings two people closer, a dialogue that enriches you and engenders a deep sense of mutuality and benevolence.

And, as I'm writing here, I'm beginning to feel a little a better, recalling the Arabic proverb: yom asal, yom basal, which means, one day honey, one day onion, so maybe tomorrow, or even today, my yom basal will turn into yom asal.

Actually, I came here to talk about something else that may be connected to the feeling of emptiness and a heavy heart and poor sleep. It looks like I may be pregnant, my period is late, almost three weeks late, and my sister is already talking about doctor appointments, saying I must soon go see a doctor who'll be supervising the progression of my pregnancy. She calls me with advice and instructions, what to eat or not to eat (avoid cabbage!), stop smoking, don't drink alcohol, and I dutifully say, Yes, of course.

The strange coincidence is that about a month ago Monsieur says to me that maybe it's time we start thinking about getting pregnant, and I say that I don't feel like traveling with a swollen tummy and morning sickness (we're planning a trip to Europe later this summer/fall), and I offer a couple of other reasons, like, the move back to New York, finding an apartment, and so on, but we agree not to use contraceptives and have intercourse twice in the middle of my cycle when an egg is released and, depending on her mood, allows sperm to enter and deliver its content into her center.

And so, my period is late, and at first, I didn't digest or worry about it. I didn't even consider the possibility that I was pregnant, telling myself that I was late because of stress. But! A few days ago, as I prepared to fall asleep, I did begin to digest and to believe, and I panicked, worrying, Oh, my God, what will I do with a baby, how will I remember to feed it (babies cry when they're hungry, my sister wisely reminded me the following day when I told her I was late and may be pregnant), and then, as soon as I told her, something in my psyche changed, and I'm now walking around with my tummy thrust forward, stroking it all the time, with something close to pride, checking to see how big it's getting and if I'm "showing," already seeing myself as a mother, and I patiently listen to my sister and even ask questions, and already there's a feeling of alert excitement about the prospect of exchanging "experiences" with mothers and pregnant women everywhere. It is overwhelming and scary, but many

47

have done it and I can, too. Monsieur is kind of
subdued, cautiously happy, he says, because he, too, is
a worrier, and he'll be happy only when the baby
arrives, and we are papa and mama.

Meanwhile, since in my mind I'm pregnant, I
allow myself to eat nonstop. In this, too, my sister
came to the rescue and, using herself as an example,
said I'd be back to my normal weight a couple of weeks
after giving birth. And so, all day yesterday, like a
magnet, I was drawn to the fridge for intermittent
handfuls of soy nuts, almonds, walnuts, sunflower and
pumpkin seeds, as well as raisins, and slices of apple,
banana, and peach. I ate all day, and this after trying to
starve myself (and my baby?) to lose the excess five
pounds I had gained. I ate all day and did no work,
except the laundry which doesn't count as "work," and
lying on the couch and reading and stroking my belly.

I've been away for many months, and you, my dear,
were packed in a box, albeit in good company—with
a few of my bedside books. And, of course, a lot has
happened, the trip to Europe, the move back to New
York. And the old year ended, and a new one began. It
took us a while, but we finally found a good apartment
in the old neighborhood—East Ninth Street—and,
reading the nonsense I wrote here last about
pregnancies and motherhood: well, nothing doing! In
the end, I got my period, no babies or swelling
tummies, I'm as skinny as ever.

Still, there was a moment of sadness, of a letdown, when my period came, after weeks of physical discomfort, watching my weight steadily rise and imagining myself heavy with child, already planning in my mind how we will change things to accommodate the new person in our lives. Wallowing in daydreams, I imagined everyone rallying to my side, and my eyes swelled with tears of gratitude. Those—females only—who made it into the delivery room were assigned specific roles: one to hold my hand and tell me to breathe, another to welcome the baby's arrival with her home movie camera, and yet another shooting stills. At first, I wasn't sure I'd want so many people and cameras in the room, but then I thought that my daughter/son would like to have their arrival documented on film, and I allowed them all to be present.

Now I'm back in the city, back to my old self, to my old friends, back to feeling that I am where I need to be. Monsieur and I, though, are still up and down, we'll see what time brings. Now I have to rush out, but I do hope to write here more often, embark on a new discipline of work, with a calm and patient heart and mind, and eyes and ears open and attentive to everyone around me. By the way, since I no longer bother you with Squabbles and No Sex, I've decided to name you: Diary of a Pupa. There, you have a name. And, I'm counting on you to do your job, i.e., discipline me to write regularly, even if it's only a few minutes of writing down what goes on in my head.

I actually enjoy writing in this book. I actually enjoy sitting here and writing. The novel is done, and I put it aside for now to let it cool, like freshly baked bread before you attempt to slice it. In the meantime, I'll go back to my drafts of short stories and see what's what. They say beginnings are hard, but for how long would I be "beginning?" Still, every day is a beginning. Every getting up from the desk and going to the bathroom and back to the desk is a beginning. But, don't be a smartass, Annette. You already know that the only real difficulty when it comes to beginning is the "thinking" about beginning. If you go to the desk and seat yourself and pick up a pen, you're on your way.

I didn't mean to go on like this, but the fact that I did is a pleasant surprise. I think I'll stop now and read for a while and then go to sleep. Monsieur, of course, is already in dreamland. To his credit: he rises early, around five or six in the morning.

Very eventful day yesterday. Monsieur and I went out and bought lumber and got to work, building shelves for our books which have been packed away in boxes for too long. Monsieur also built a small desk for me by the window in the bedroom. This is to be my "corner" where I can leave my stuff without worrying about Monsieur moving things around because he needs the desk; he has his own desk by the window in the living room. I've been quite productive, doing some work yesterday and also this morning. I woke up and was out of bed by eight o'clock which is quite

50

impressive. I'm changing my "habits" and I'm very pleased with myself.

Another habit gone with the wind: cigarettes. I do smoke an occasional cigarette that I bum off Monsieur, one or two a day, but that's it; no more puffing and coughing for me. I look out the window and it's gray, and it looks even grayer because our windowpanes need a diligent and thorough cleaning. Will have to poke Monsieur and remind him that cleaning windows is his job. That's life. I may come back later.

I forgot to tell you that both Monsieur and I have jobs: mine is part-time, his is fulltime, but his is only for the time being, until he lands a teaching position. I, as proofreader at the law firm where Lucy is a proofreader. She recommended me, I went for an interview, and I'm now employed. It's not too boring, and they pay well. Monsieur works for a company that puts together conferences for executives, mostly in finance, he does the research and helps organize and call upon experts in the field and negotiate the speaker's fee.

His job takes him to hotels around town where the conferences take place, the other day it was the Plaza Hotel, where, he says, except for the food, everything was quite dull. An assemblage of 140 financiers—mostly suited men and a few suited women—most of them suitably bored. Surprisingly, or not so surprisingly, quite a number of them left after lunch, others fell asleep in the lecture hall, and some simply didn't show up, even though their companies had paid a hefty $850 for a one-day seminar. I don't understand this kind of waste, or, actually, I do. These people, and the institutions they work for, freely throw $$ at another well-to-do company—in this case Monsieur's company—and business as usual. It's not right, but again, this is part of modern life, it's the façade that counts and keeping your name on people's lips.

Enough of this. Time to read a bit and then out the door and go to work. It's a sunny day outside, and, before long, summer will be here, and bulky winter clothes out of the way and out of sight.

Have not been as diligent as promised, but am willing to forgive myself, offering excuses, such as: readjusting to my city, walking everywhere, feasting my eyes, constant movement and people everywhere, of all color and shade, exuberant outfits, and not even one vanilla face. Last night sat with Lucy and Jamie in a small café on First Avenue, they had tables on the sidewalk and that's where we sat even though it was chilly. I felt so lucky and alive, watching, with loving eyes, humanity go past, a constant stream of limbs, colors, bits of dialogue, and faces, faces, faces alive with the moment, characters of every imaginable shape, age, and idiosyncrasy.

And the three of us were part of the general excitement, talking—shouting really—and laughing, discussing life and death and everything in between.

We lamented the lying, mechanical sex scenes coming out of Hollywood, where couples go at each other, their passion knows no bounds, tearing each other's clothes, the man always gets an erection, he never ejaculates prematurely, and the woman always comes. "Ah, the beautiful life in the movies," Lucy shouted, and we ordered another round of drinks.

Later, when we parted, Lucy and Jamie took the train and, as I walked home, an impromptu hymn to New York began to play in my head, a hymn to the people, young and old, streaming past me, and when I got home I found Monsieur asleep in bed, and I felt a rush of affection for him, sleeping like a baby while his wife is cavorting in the streets, so I kissed him on the forehead and went back to the living room, surfed through a few channels, and then got myself in bed and fell asleep instantly.

The Pope was shot yesterday, right in St. Peter's Square—we are all in shock. The would-be assassin is a Turkish fugitive—an escaped prisoner who two years ago killed a journalist. Some suspect the KGB is involved. And, for me, this is yet another marker on our way to self-destruction. Ever since I heard the news, I've been carrying around a strange mood, a kind of doomsday anxiety about life on earth. Sometimes it feels as though people in the so-called developed world are sick and tired of all the comforts and arrogance they've accumulated, but that's all they've got and are familiar with, and it's too late to give it up. And yet, the more they accumulate, the greater the burden, the fear and the worry they'd lose it. Maybe, without being aware of it, they're looking for a fresh start, for something that would restore meaning to their lives, to their everyday, maybe the world needs to explode and go back to the beginning, to the tohu va bohu in Genesis, and start again from scratch.

But I don't want the world to explode. I want to live. I'm constantly hungry and on the lookout for good news of any kind. I was at work when we heard about the Pope, and it was yet another confirmation that yes, indeed, good news is rare these days. Right now I feel that the world is doomed, and it will all begin in my stomach because for me the world is me and I'll be destroyed together with the world and everything in it. I don't think we can escape it so there's no point running to the hills like groups of survivalists are doing. Let these defeatist thoughts and fears evaporate and let us enjoy this spring, and the next.

Also, I've been trying not to admit it, but it's possible that I don't feel like myself these past few days because I've done no significant work. I'm procrastinating again, it upsets me, and I torture myself with bad thoughts and admonitions. I tell myself what's the point of working, writing, if we're all doomed. And then I tell myself I must change my attitude, starting tomorrow, and then another tomorrow comes, and another. I want the Pope to recover! And I want good people of action to wake up and steer us toward a more constructive and peaceful path. Amen.

Had a disturbing/realistic/close to home dream last night. In the dream I'm reading a book about a couple that fights and bickers all the time. They may or may not have committed a crime, and in order to clear their names they must talk to the judge. But they're so prideful and stubborn, they persist in their silence, and therefore the frustrated judge finds them guilty and condemns them to death. I'm upset, and I talk to Monsieur, asking if he can explain this business to me, and Monsieur says: "It's only a novel," and I say, "No, it's a memoir. I want to know how the woman felt when she was led to her death." In a simulation, I'm blindfolded and led to death in her stead, and the arm of the male guard leading me comforts me greatly.

Rose this morning at 8:30am—the latest in quite a while. I was extremely tired, couldn't get my eyes to open, but now, after a shower, and with coffee and a cigarette (yes, am smoking again, but only five a day), am slowly waking. From up here, the street below seems quiet, peaceful, and the fog endows everything with an aura of suspended stillness. And, if there is movement—be it a tree branch or a human—it is a slow-motion ballet. I must leave now and get myself to the office.

I've worked all morning and am stopping now, filled with admiration for myself. Later today I may type what I longhanded. We'll see. I've also discovered that I work much better without smoke rising from between my delicate fingers, clouding my eyes and irritating my throat. I MUST REMEMBER that smoking is forbidden at this desk.

Later in the afternoon. Received a warm letter from my mother, so I wrote back immediately and also answered all the other letters waiting for an answer. I was going to do it tomorrow but doing it today will open up time tomorrow for work. I'm going to clean the apartment now, but first, a word of wisdom from Henri-Frédéric Amiel's Journal: "We only find rest in effort, as the flame only finds existence in combustion."

I'm up again, and today, finally, the sun is out; it has been foggy and cloudy for the last few days. From up here, I can hear the wind pummeling our building, which means that this is not a full-fledged spring day, but half and half. Enough with the weather. I am very happy with the new beginning I have for the novel, and today's sitting, God willing, will be productive. I've also decided I must exercise ten minutes every morning, jogging from room to room, and obeying any other inspired move my body in motion dictates, and then, if time allows, start the day by reading a poem or two.

Today would/could have been a writing day, but I'm having gum surgery in a couple of hours so writing is not in the schedule, but I think I'll be able to read. After the first surgery on my poor gums, I took two painkillers and slept all day. This time I'll take one pill and see what happens. Yesterday on the news we watched Menachem Begin give a speech, promising the "enemy" that Israel "shall be ready" for the next war. Never will we suffer another Yom Kippur, he announced in his usual style. Listening to and watching him, I got sick to my stomach: why not be ready for the next peace negotiations. Right now I'd better get out of bed and get myself ready to leave the house and go uptown to my periodontist.

The morning after. This time, surgery wasn't as bad as the first one. Last night I ate like a horse—but a slow horse. I was starved. I'm not as swollen as last time, or, at least, it doesn't show as much because this time it's on the lower jaw, whereas before it was the upper jaw and the swelling bloomed smack center on my face. I can't concentrate on writing now. I sit here, drowsy, looking out the window, and no, or minimal, activity in the brain.

As boring and "adult" as it may seem, I've decided that routine (i.e., discipline) is the most important thing for someone like me. And so, I have worked out a schedule and have every intention to stick to it, if not always to the same exact routine, then at least to the framework of a routine. I get out of bed at 7:10am, go into the shower, and am back in bed at 7:30, writing. As soon as summer is here and it's warm, I'll write at my desk, naked of course. I could do it today, write at my desk, because, for a change, it's a little warm this morning, and it's sunny. But I'll stay in bed.

You wouldn't guess it from this upbeat beginning, but I had a terrible evening yesterday. It started at work and, without getting into asinine details, I got upset courtesy of Sheila (the "supervisor" of us minions in the office), and when I came home, Monsieur wasn't here, and, morose and stewing, I allowed myself to wallow in my swamp, and, when he finally arrived, I vented my misery at him. When I got home, I thought that maybe I should sit down and write out my anger in you, little book, but I didn't. Instead, I let it fester and grow bigger and bigger until it became a monster, and when Monsieur came home, the monster got loose and rose to meet him. I was horrible. I hated myself while and after I said what I said.

It's unbearable when something like this happens. I lose/concede control and say things I never meant to say. But luckily Monsieur sometimes is capable of patience, and after I was done ranting, I realized what I'd done. I apologized and he forgave.

And, of course, the fact that my face is still a bit achy and swollen doesn't inspire a cheerful mood either. But, I have to learn to control my temper. There are many things I have to do. I have to learn to ignore inconsistent people like Sheila who go from extreme to extreme with no warning and no apparent reason. I have to learn to ignore such people, instead of trying to figure out why they act the way they do. Lucy, who got me the job, says that Sheila is consistent, she's evil, and Lucy may be right, she certainly knows Sheila longer and better than I do.

Still, I believe that Sheila fluctuates between civil and uncivil, no one is constant, we all have our "moments," but Monsieur says that I tend to embellish situations and people, and that it's time I shed my "Pollyanna" view of the world. He could be right, but I should also listen to myself and consider and acknowledge the fact that I'm overly touchy and take everything to heart.

Also, I grew up with a father who daily recited quotes from The Book of Proverbs, and from Pirkei Avot, trying to teach me to always choose the right path: "Say little and do much"; "Who is wise? One who learns from every man. Who is strong? One who overpowers his inclinations. Who is rich? One who is satisfied with his lot. Who is honorable? One who honors his fellows." And, most importantly, the proverb warning about the harm of idle gossip: "Death and life are in the power of the tongue: and they that love it shall eat the fruit thereof." And Maimonides, too, was a regular presence, and his famous—"The more necessary a thing is for living beings, the more easily it is found and cheaper it is; the less necessary it is, the rarer and dearest it is"—our cherished incantation.

And so, I have to conclude that I'm an obsolete idiot who lives in her father's world and doesn't pay enough attention to "reality." An idiot who always wants to put people at ease, and she tries so hard she sometimes achieves the opposite result. But, in a way, I prefer to live as a Pollyanna, rather than fill my head with bad thoughts and suspicions about people, because such thoughts and suspicions only poison the heart and the mind, and whatever you project onto others becomes yours to own.

Later. And while I'm yapping about this and that, I hear on the radio that a third IRA prisoner died. This is too... I don't have the words. These young people—they're my age and younger—actually starve themselves. They die a slow and painful death for a free Ireland. They actually go on a hunger strike and are allowed to die. The courage and determination it takes stir my heart. Sooner or later the British will have to get the message and leave Ireland while *they* are still alive. Sometimes I think that the world is such a crazy place to be in, maybe it's best to try and avoid the news, which is hard to do.

Advice to myself: A short story should be written as if you're short of breath, and you're writing everything down quickly as if fearing that if you don't write it down immediately, it will vanish. And this is Thursday night, and I got home from work two hours ago, and I am tired. This week has been a rough one, but on the way home, I said to myself, in a kind of singsong: Don't forget to take pleasure in people! And when the singsong ended, the thought came: Remember, some people are nice, and some people are not so nice. But it also happens that a nice person may be not so nice on certain days, and a not so nice person may be nice on certain days.

My sister came to me in a good and strange dream! I'm in my living room, dressed to go out. I look out the window as if to see what the weather is like, and suddenly I'm laughing, laughing. My sister is in the room with me. I tell her: "Look, I can't stop laughing." My eyes are half shut, like I'm waking up, and she, also laughing, comes near me and peers into my face as if trying to figure out what's going on with me.

Actually, now that I think of it, there's a photograph of the two of us, I'm about six and she's about five, we're both wearing dresses, so it must have been a holiday. I'm smiling at the camera, while she, a bit shorter than me, ignores the camera completely and peers into my face with a questioning smile. Funny! I'll have to write and tell her about the dream.

How comforting it is, sitting like this in the morning, naked and clean and warm under the covers, propped against pillows, listening to classical music and to the occasional interruptions of the presenter, who, thankfully, has a soothing and pleasant voice that perfectly complements the music. He could never host a rock 'n roll program, and I wonder if he was advised at the start of his career to choose classical, or if it was his preference all along. It's not terribly important, but things like that do engage me sometimes, and Monsieur gets annoyed, saying he doesn't understand why I ask about things that no one bothers their head about, let alone care enough to ask a question rather than let it quietly die. Ah, well.

Got up later than usual, feeling grumpy and out of sorts. I woke up early, at seven, and then lingered and fell asleep again, and when I finally got myself out of bed, my head felt heavy, my face puffy, and a fuzzy gray cloud settled in my soul. And, it's a beautiful day out! Resolution: as soon as I open my eyes, I must jump out of bed instead of lingering/ brooding/ trying to remember dreams.

And now, sitting here, still struggling to climb out from under, I wish I lived near the ocean so I could walk barefoot on the beach early in the morning, waking up to sky and water, and then, ready and eager to start my day, I'd walk home, calm and content.

And, what's also on my mind is the letter I received yesterday from my sister, telling me, among other things, that a baby from me would make my father very happy. She says that a child from me equals a dozen from her, that's how badly he wants a grandchild from his eldest daughter.

Monsieur and I looked at each other and said, Okay, let's have a baby, but, of course, nothing will come of it, just like when we tried last year. I don't think we're ready for parenthood. I know that when I look at the "romantic" side of it, I like the idea of having a baby, but when I think about what it takes to actually raise that child, fear and doubts replace excitement.

My sister says we don't know what we're missing, and I know she is right. I know that to bring a new being into the world is a unique and special experience, even if fears and worries and difficulties are part of it. But I don't trust myself. I'm a worrier, and if had a child I wouldn't let it out of my sight. Also, I worry that my fear about having a baby has more to do with my uncertainty about the future, namely, my marriage. It is possible that if I were married to a different person, I would want a baby as much as my father and my sister want it. And, of course, my mother, who never pressures me, but I know she'll be thrilled. I'm also thinking that the same may be true for Monsieur, that if he were married to another, the two of them would be good parents.

There's no hot water this morning so I can't take a shower, which means I'm still half asleep. Today is a day off for me, and I want to sit in the sun. The last three days were sunny and inviting, and yet, I remained at my desk, working, both here and at the office, while others, less burdened than me, got to worship the sun. Today I'll join them. I'd better get out of bed and have breakfast and slowly wake up.

Later. We finally got our hot water back, and life is normal again. Today, as planned, I took a day off. I went out for a walk and sat in the park and read, exposing my white self to the sun. Now I'm still white in most parts, and red in others. Monsieur is in the living room, and I'm at my small desk, staring out the window and trying to think of something that may be worth a mention in this notebook, but nothing concrete surfaces in this quiet, lazy day.

I'm back. Left for a while to read and I'm back, staring out the window again, watching the sun as it gets lower and lower in the sky, and redder and redder. I've been quite pleased with myself these past few days, pleased that I've managed to discipline myself to jump out of bed at hours which were inconceivable at former times, times that now seem distant. Jumping out of bed and working every day, and therefore allowing myself a day off. I'm bursting with energy, with projects, with good thoughts, and I feel I'm alive. And now I'll stop and continue to read.

A few nights ago, Monsieur and I walked through Washington Square Park and noticed a small gathering of people, two ambulances, police, and we approached the circle to see what it was all about. A man lying on the ground was hooked up to various types of medical equipment as the paramedics were pumping oxygen into him and applying chest compressions, trying to revive him. Apparently, the guy—young and black and large—was happily dancing when, all of a sudden, he collapsed. And so we stood in complete silence, watching science at work, hoping the medics will save the guy. Suddenly, a man next to us, said: "It's a scam," and walked away. It was weird. The man, white and wearing a suit, seemed to be in his thirties and, for some reason, was angry.

After pumping the guy's chest for quite a while, they put him in one of the ambulances and drove off. Afterward, on the way home, I told Monsieur I thought that the policemen, who were watching the whole thing and probably knew the guy, a regular in the park, were maybe thinking to themselves—just like the angry man muttering "It's a scam"—that the guy wasn't worth all the trouble, all this fine and expensive machinery.

I'm not sure they thought it, but there must be a special relationship based on hate and fear between the police and the black men in the park, and I'm more and more aware of it ever since I saw a policeman shoot a black man, then shooting him again, in his back!, after he was already on the ground, wounded or dead from the first bullet. I saw a lot of hate and cold blood in the way the policeman aimed his gun to the ground where the man lay motionless and shot him twice more. In the eyes of the police, of course, he deserved to die: he went after the policeman with a hammer, or so they claimed, and was a regular in the "notorious" Union Square Park.

Pascal says that we don't live in the present but look to the future or the past. He explains it by saying that oftentimes the present hurts. Not to contradict Pascal, but I think that people look to the future, or the past, because the present doesn't "exist," the present is our breath-by-breath existence, it's in motion, we cannot grasp or apprehend it. When we're in a bad mood, or worse, we don't look to the future, or the past, we're sunk, we're sinking in misery, in a constant unremitting present, until the veil lifts and we're ourselves again, until the next "attack" comes. In the future, of course.

Monsieur went to the movies with John, and I stayed home, saying I'm tired and not in the mood to go out. I stayed home and read and pampered myself with munchies, fruit and camembert and slices of dark crusty bread I buy by the pound from the Ukrainian meat store on Second Avenue.

My pleasures may be small, but intense, and private. I forget now who said it, but it's something to the effect that if you love a book, you love the author, and I do love Henri-Frédéric Amiel who whispers to me: "Let mystery have its place in you; do not be always turning up your whole soil with the ploughshare of self-examination, but leave a little fallow corner in your heart ready for any seed the winds may bring, and reserve a nook of shadow for the passing bird." Amiel has taken permanent possession of a corner on my desk, and in my heart.

I'm not in the greatest of moods this morning, but I'm going to work against it, so I don't ruin an entire day for myself and waste it. Later, I'm going to my periodontist and have that awful white dressing taken off my gums. I have to have two more surgeries, and then my mouth will be healthy, I hope. I, who never went to doctors and never had any surgeries or treatments, am all of a sudden enmeshed in gum treatments and teeth and health and other miscellaneous concerns. Does this mean I'm getting "old?" I'd better get to work now and stop wallowing in nonsense.

I'm again in a "bad mood"—funny words—and the weather outside is not much help: it's grim and gray. The dollar is down overseas, said the announcer, and that's what I'll be hearing all day at work: the dollar is down, the D-mark is weak. Did I say? I took on a temporary, two-month assignment, proofreading for a financial news outfit one day a week—Thursdays.

I'm in a strange mood this morning, and I do know why, but I'm not going to tell you. It's the same old reason, so, in a way, you do know. It's an old problem with a new urgency, my body wants and needs what it wants and needs, and I'm sick and tired of denying it and myself. I could, of course, take on a lover, but then, what's the point of being married. That's it for now. I may come back later tonight if the spirit so moves me.

I've been basking in the sun in the park for about two hours, reading and gazing, reading and gazing. But I did manage to do some work early in the morning, which is good!

Yesterday I came home and found Monsieur cleaning the apartment, but not just cleaning—he gave it a thorough and furious tidying, maybe as a rebuke to me, and the apartment looks as if a storm went through it. Thankfully, he left my desk alone. He was in a "mood" and hardly said a word to me. Toward evening he warmed up and we had a nice, chatty dinner. We went to the movies and saw "Atlantic City" and everything was still fine. When we came out of the theater, Monsieur was in a "mood" again—he didn't like the movie, he was bored, and it annoyed him that I enjoyed it. And, of course, we fought. And that's what makes life so uniquely rewarding: repetition.

Incidentally, I read in the park that Easterners deal with boredom in a totally different way than we Westerners do. When they feel "bored" they do not reach for a book or for something to do, they do not look for a distraction hoping to alleviate the boredom, they let the boredom take its course until it is fully experienced and spent.

On the other hand, they do think of ways to rejuvenate their days, which is basically what I've done not too long ago when I changed my sleeping/ smoking/ writing habits. I wasn't bored, I was miserable with the way things were. Now, even when I don't work, at least I know I didn't spend the day in bed. And I do write here, if not every day, then often. This notebook is part of my "rejuvenation program."

And, Monsieur and I are not talking. War has been declared, and we're keeping to it, respectfully, as befits two seasoned antagonists.

Later. Monsieur came over to my desk and apologized, and I punched him in the arm, and he punched me back, and I called him names, and now we feel much better.

Busy Saturday morning. I got up at 7:15 and haven't even eaten my yogurt yet. As usual, I took my shower, exercised a bit, and then, instead of making breakfast, I came here to note something down for a story I began last night, "The Girl TinTin," but instead I opened you, little book.

A few minutes ago I said to Monsieur: "Why don't we go out and do something fun for a change? Let's take half a day off." He objected a bit at first, saying he had work to do, but after I said he could work in the afternoon, he agreed. We decided to go to the Museum of Natural History and come back home around 4pm and go to our desks. We both need more relaxation and fun-time in our lives. We're always busy doing things, as if afraid we'd lose our turn in line if we don't keep up. Which is an absurd way to live.

I envy people who do whatever they need to do slowly, who take their time when doing this and that. I always rush through "chores" as if possessed, instead of enjoying the work, the devotion to one thing at a time. I wish I had the presence of mind—presence in the sense of present to the task at hand, be it sewing a button! I was never this time-haunted, I was never so driven. Maybe this is what they mean when they talk about reaching adulthood, responsible adulthood.

Whatever it is, I think I contracted this adulthood condition from Monsieur. I'm going to eat now because my stomach is here, but before that I'll write down the paragraph for TinTin, which appeared in my mind, fully formed and wrapped like a gift, when I was exercising in front of the mirror.

I'm in bed again, after showering and jogging from room to room and exercising/ stretching, and, in the process, exorcising demons. It's awful out—gray and rainy and chilly. So I'm in bed with you, my loyal companion.

The other day we didn't feel like going all the way uptown to the museum and went to SoHo instead and walked around, in and out of galleries, feasting our eyes. Then we sat in a café on the sidewalk and the wind sprayed our faces and jackets with prickly brown sugar grains from the quaint lidless bowl on the table. Then we came home, and I worked for a while.

Last night David, one of Monsieur's colleagues, called and we went out and met him in a bar for drinks and chicken wings, and, after we said our goodbyes, Monsieur and I, suddenly hungry again, went in search of a restaurant, it was late, almost eleven, but we found an Indian restaurant on Sixth Street that still served food, be it just for two wanderers, as we were the only people in the place except for the owners and waiters. We ate, and again, old reliable Visa paid for it. What would this country come to if it weren't for these handsome plastic cards?

Monsieur and I discussed our misunderstandings and tried to come up with a formula to help prevent them, but we know from past episodes that formulas don't work for us, and neither do the sincerest promises and intentions. But, we don't despair. Then we came home, exhausted, and went to bed. Tonight we're going to Broadway to see "Piaf." TDF sent us half-price tickets and we figured, why not, even though we prefer Off or Off-Off Broadway. Ciao.

This morning, for some reason, my thoughts went back to Paris, to Jaime, who was in love with me and studied medicine, and who today must be a married doctor with two or three kids. But then, maybe not.

It occurs to me that Jaime came to mind because last night we finally saw a good Broadway show— "Piaf." It's the first time that I left a Broadway theater ecstatic. Actually, the second. A few years ago we saw Ralph Richardson and John Gielgud in Pinter's "No Man's Land" and that, too, was a memorable production, directed by Peter Hall. Just to see these two giants on the stage would have been enough.

But back to Jane Lapotaire who was an exquisite and amazing Piaf. The strange thing is that the show is not attracting large audiences, for Monsieur and I got our tickets through TDF, and we sat in the first row, privy to every drop of sweat, to the white spray of spittle from lips, to the accumulation of saliva in the mouth, and the tense throat muscles.

During the intermission, a funny thing happened. Monsieur and I went outside, and out of the blue there appeared a young man in a black suit who proceeded to set up shop in front of the theater, and people began to gather. Monsieur and I were directly in front of him—first row again—and watched him turn on his tape recorder and begin a mime show, a marionette-like mime show—his feet were rooted to the ground and he was swaying back and forth and sideways, while swinging his arms very fast, which was amazing to watch, the way he had transformed himself into a mechanical doll. It didn't last long, and he soon passed his hat around, and then disappeared, probably in a hurry to catch another intermission at one of the nearby theaters.

But then, as soon as he disappeared, a pushcart appeared and took the mime's spot and offered its goodies to the still assembled crowd: pretzels. And then a funny thought came to me, and I told Monsieur, and we both stood there laughing hysterically. I said to him: "Imagine us standing here, watching the mime, he leaves, and then the pretzel man appears for a few minutes, and then he leaves, and an ice cream wagon appears, and so on, an unstoppable cavalcade of tempting goods."

It doesn't sound so funny now, but last night the image was so vivid, so surreal, it was hilarious. Now I'll read for a while, David Markson's *Springer's Progress*.

Hard to believe, but Hitler was a cute-looking baby, with large, dark eyes, and silky dark hair. Baby Adolf looks innocent, like any baby, and could easily be mistaken for a cute Jewish baby-girl. People who want to find omens in the face may attach significance to the fact that the head seems wrong for the body, the symmetry seems off somehow, and we, humans, do associate symmetry with health and beauty; and to the fact that there's no trace of a smile on the baby's face—in fact, he looks startled, even annoyed at the people who stand outside the frame and try to make him smile. The photograph was taken around 1890, so baby Adolf is about one year old.

And Monsieur bought a new machine, a PC, and he's absolutely in love with it, and proud of it, too. He tries to convince me of its many wonders, but I have no patience for it, my mind goes blank when he tries to explain. I prefer to continue to handwrite and to type on my cute, pale-green manual portable Hermes. He says I must keep up with the times, and I say that no, I don't have to, but, of course, there's a small chiding voice in my head that repeats the same words, urging me to keep up with the times, so, a new kind of conflict and more self-doubting.

I'm quite practiced when it comes to beating up on myself and filling my heart with misery. This is something that you and I, my little book, already know. Too much is going on in my little brain, too much confusion, too many thoughts, dilemmas, and doubts. The only escape is to look to the future and daydream (Pascal again), fantasizing about a glorious and satisfying time—another thing I'm quite good at. Enough. But, one more word: I have to rediscover in myself the joy, the zest for life.

This morning, alone in bed, I didn't jump out and rush to the shower, but lingered, and in the haze of half-sleep, a gallery of poised faces appeared under my eyelids, faces I didn't recognize, and yet, empathized with. Tranquil face after tranquil face of youngish women, as if posing for a photograph, a hint of a smile on their relaxed features. And then it was one face, the face of an old woman, with deep lines running down her cheeks and around her mouth and eyes, and I suddenly recognized her face as very much like my own, but I was not mortified, she was smiling at me, a gentle and diffident smile, and I smiled back, taking her in. She reminded me a little of my mother, even though my mother isn't that old and hardly has any wrinkles, and I realized that I was looking at a face that I would see in the mirror if I live long enough.

This is a slow morning even though I got up early. The hot water was slow to come, and I spent over half an hour in the bathroom, doing this and that, waiting for the water to be nice and hot, but it didn't happen, so I ended up taking a lukewarm shower, more luke than warm—the delights of living in the city—and I'm still carrying with me feelings of frustration and guilt because last night I had too much wine and smoked six cigarettes, which is hateful.

Annette, Annette, when will you learn. Still, I'm in a fairly decent mood, only feeling bad about yesterday, and looking forward to today, determined not to drink. At least, not to excess. Now I'm going to feed my fish (did I say? We got a medium-size aquarium and a few cute goldfish living in it), then feed myself, and then go to work. It does no good sitting here, brooding about yesterday.

What a day. Clear and sunny and a nice breeze to cool things off. I begin to sound like a radio announcer, or a chipper weatherman. Yesterday worked for a few hours then sat in the sun. Last night Monsieur surprised us both, cooking a delicious Spanish dinner and, for dessert, he served a baked rice pudding cookie with whipped cream. We watched the Tony awards, and when my Piaf, Jane Lapotaire, won the Best Actress Award, I applauded the screen and blew air kisses. There's a sweetness in her face and voice, and your heart opens to her and remains open for as long as you watch her.

I took a "vacation" today and stayed in bed till nine o'clock. Now I'm sitting here, looking out the window, still a little groggy and sleepy.

And Monsieur just came to my desk, and I rose from the chair and we had a fist fight. We'll be going out for a walk in a few minutes and fresh air should wake me up.

Later. We came back from the walk, I had lunch, I read, and I'm still feeling kind of mild and lazy. What's the matter with me? Why can't I discipline myself to sit down and work, be it only for an hour?

So many thoughts and ideas and worries mix in my head and, of course, doubts. I procrastinate, or, more precisely, I read and don't write.

I'm sitting here, wishing I didn't have to worry about chores, like cleaning the house, and this got me thinking about those who don't have creative aspirations, a creative impulse, or a need for an outlet, and I'm asking myself how do they go through life, raising a family, getting up in the morning, going to work, coming home, going to a movie, to the theater, they keep busy, they "accumulate" experiences and social events, but what are their deeper, their "after" thoughts? When they're alone with themselves, or even when surrounded by family and friends, do they allow existential apprehension, do they wonder—where do I go from here? What's my higher purpose?

For some, this is where God and religion enter, but those who are not religious, what about them? And, the more pressing question right now: Where do *I* go from here? Will my work ever count for something? "There is nothing new under the sun" said the wisest of men, but even the familiar can be made new if you have it in you to sit down and make it yours. And, again, brain buzzing with plans, and I must stop buzzing with plans and get to work!

Hi there. I'm making breakfast. Have been super industrious this morning: cleaning and laundry behind me, and still have the whole day to look forward to. Breakfast first.

Finished my breakfast and now here back with you. Last night we went to see "Tosca" together with 200,000 people who settled on the Great Lawn in Central Park, ready to partake of food and listen to opera, all of us, like one large family, sprawled on blankets on the grass under the stars with food and wine and talking and laughing and then absolute silence when the orchestra struck the first notes of the overture. And as I lay on the blanket and shut my eyes, I was suddenly filled with gratitude, envisioning a world where communication was still possible among peoples and that the end of the world is not here yet, and that hate and violence can be put away in a bin with other past cruelties and rubbish.

During intermission, I stood up and looked around, wanting to see all the people who had gathered here, all strangers, but really not strangers, and I was struck again by the abundance and variety of foods Americans bring to picnics. Not cold cuts—which is always the easiest solution—but real food, cooked and served from real bowls, even pans, and all kinds of breads, fruits, pastries, and cookies and, of course, plenty of wine. Some even brought small tables and tablecloths and a flower or two in a small vase. I thought how good it was to be there, mellow and accepting, looking around and watching all these people, together, celebrating the music, themselves, and their neighbors on the grass.

And, listening to the opera I heard the love of the singers in their voices, and the thought came to me that opera singers are the performers who truly share a gift with us commoners. I'm not taking away from actors or dancers, but with opera singers you forget about technique and drive, it is pure love that you hear, a love that richly comes through in the voice, from deep inside. And this is what happened last night under the stars, the singers bestowing their gift on us. Amazing.

Had a good, productive morning, I cleaned a bit, went down to the supermarket, worked at my desk, and soon will go down again, this time to the park, to sit and read—it's too beautiful out to stay indoors.

Yesterday, when we came home, Monsieur and I were carrying grocery bags, our hands effectively "tied up." As we were about to enter the building, Tom, who lives in the building and is one of the handymen, was coming out with his small white poodle. Instead of holding the outside door for us, Tom let it slam in our faces and continued to stand there, blocking our way to the door and looking down at his feet where the dog, like Tom, stood and waited.

Obviously, Tom was drunk. I think he simply didn't see us even though he responded to our "hello." He was elsewhere, with the fumes of alcohol, and with his dog. We fumbled for keys, went around him, and entered the building. While we waited for the elevator, Tom was still standing in the same spot on the other side of the door, and my heart went out to him and the dog as the realization hit me that all Tom had was his dog and his bottle. He's around fifty-sixty years old, and no family, as far as I know. Before the poodle he had a large dog, a rambunctious puppy that was still growing and getting bigger and bigger. Tom gave the dog away because he couldn't handle it. For a while he was without a dog, until recently when he got this small, frightened poodle.

On the news: People are being executed in Iran, and, in a way, the circle is complete. Khomeini took over and began executing people in the name of the Islamic Revolution, very much like the Shah who had executed people in the name of progress. I don't see the difference, the awful result is the same, except that Khomeini reinstated public executions. And now Khomeini is after people who supported him, people like Bani-Sadr who helped bring about the old nut's "revolution." They've already executed nearly a thousand citizens, and Iranians are now cursing (in private) the day they allowed this fanatic to come back, welcoming him and his entourage with open hearts and arms.

What happened to me this morning, God only knows. I'm not political, but hearing that people are being executed because they're "leftists" or "Zionists" gets my blood boiling, especially when done by a regime that took over another regime because the latter was arresting and torturing people. The new regime seems to be doing even better: quick executions by hanging or firing squads. The pious duplicity is what kills me. It seems from afar that they're all insane and fanatic, but most are now trapped in their own country with no place to run, with a Fuehrer who advocates and extols marriage with a young girl as "divine blessing." One of his own four brides was ten years old when he married her. The illustrious Ayatollah goes further, saying that a man may marry a young girl, even if she's still a baby, and he may fondle her and rub his penis between her thighs, but he can consummate the marriage only when she reaches the ripe age of nine. After all, he says, the Prophet himself married a six-year-old girl.

But what's the point of railing against duplicity? Duplicity has always been here and always will be, it's a human disease, the same as base cowardice, as, for instance, when God asks Cain, "Where is Abel thy brother?" and Cain replies: "I know not: Am I my brother's keeper?" The only people who aren't infected are people like Tom, people who gave up on the system, on human society, and quietly survive on the margins.

And you, Annette, where are you in this picture? At times, I'm with Tom in his corner; at times, among the hypocrites, Annette replies. She knows that the lure of power and bloodshed animates the human soul, saints and holy men included. In fact, she doesn't believe in "saints" and "holy men." Hardcore cynicism and simple elemental brutality rule. Still, Annette says, we must also keep in mind that there are many people who may have their moments of hypocrisy, but their basic disposition is fairness and decency. And it also happens that even tyrannical hypocrites can be touched, allowing decency to knock on their hearts and ask for permission to enter, and, at times, permission is granted.

And yes, Annette also believes that she always tries to be decent and truthful, even though she's aware that this is a silly thing to aspire to in our world—you become a living walking joke. Everywhere you turn, life teaches you: better be tough and ruthless and always think of Numero Uno.

Charles, our black goldfish, hasn't been feeling well lately, and this morning we changed the water in the tank as we were told to do yesterday at the pet store. Then Monsieur picked up Charles with a small stick and brought him up to the surface, while I sprinkled food right in front of his face, practically trying to force-feed him, but Charles wouldn't eat. So, we let him be, hoping that changing the water would restore him.

And: these past few days have been perfect summer days, hot and dry and refreshing breezes, too.

It feels silly to say, Here I am again, bright and early, with my yogurt and banana, but I'll say it anyway. Here I am again with my yogurt and banana. "The Magic Flute" on WNCN, I hold a pen in my hand, and you, my book, are open before me like, well yes, a book. And Charles is not feeling better. Yesterday we noticed that the two other fish were attacking him—the bastards!—so Monsieur took him out and put him in a different bowl. I decided to call it the hospital; Charles is in hospital and, we pray, recovering.

Yesterday I worked well, and also sat and thought a lot, just sitting at the desk and thinking. I feel pretty good this morning. I woke up early, at seven o'clock, showered, exercised, and now I eat and write and will still have time to read a bit before setting out to the office. And, this afternoon, I'll get myself to the public swimming pool on Twenty-third Street.

And speaking of desk and thinking, here's Jules Renard who, in his diary, happily compares himself to a donkey: "At my desk I am like a donkey in his stall. I read and do nothing. My mind eats and ruminates."

And then there is Freud in a 1919 letter to his friend Oskar Pfister: "With me, fantasizing and working coincide; I find amusement in nothing else."

Good morning. I'm still a bit hazy, and I can't tell if I feel good or just okay. Charles died two days ago, and Monsieur and I gave him a proper, if not very dignified, burial—down the toilet. I wanted to bury him in the park, but Monsieur explained that as a creature of the sea, Charles should be sent on his way to the Great Sea via water. So we took the small bowl, the "hospital," to the bathroom, said a few solemn words of parting, and then watched Charles twirl with the current until he was gone. Unsure of what to do next, we stood there a while, a bit embarrassed, and that was it.

He was a brave fish, he was my favorite, he was black and different in shape and size from the other two goldfish. I want to believe that he died of old age and not of a disease that involved discomfort and pain.

This morning the house was cleaned in a flash, a few lines were jotted down for a story, and now I sit here, having my banana and yogurt and writing here before dashing off to a wedding. Yes, a wedding. People are getting married left and right. Michael is the groom, and the wedding is to take place on the Staten Island ferry, on one of its regular runs, which means that the wedding guests have to pay to get on the ferry and then look for the bride and the groom among the many New Yorkers and tourists who will want to go to the Statue of Liberty on the Day of Independence.

And there's a parade at eleven o'clock in Battery Park, and that's when the ferry departs, hopefully with us on it. I don't know if Michael had planned to get married on the ferry because he wanted a captain to marry them, but I do know that at one point the captain was going to marry them, but that fell through, and a minister will do the job. As for the bride Kathy, I know nothing about her, except that she met Michael six months ago and the two of them sailed on to a stormy relationship, and now, marriage. Kind of reminds me of Monsieur and me. All I can do is wish them good luck and lots of patience and forbearance.

Monsieur says I look like a small chipmunk, and I do. Had another gum surgery yesterday, and this morning, upon waking, I saw a new face in the mirror, inflamed and swollen. Yesterday afternoon, Monsieur and I saw "The Tempest" in the park. From the start it was clear that the production was dead, hopeless, and the only thing to do was to sit and feel bad for the actors who did what they could. Getting up and leaving was out of the question, as it would only add to their misery. In short, what the actors had to go

83

through in order to satisfy a director with no vision was embarrassing to watch.

Yesterday, the lawyers in the office seemed to be walking on egg-shells, and we—"the help"—also went mute. When I think about the petty power play in a run-of-the-mill law firm, I ask myself how people ever withstand and survive in institutions where power does carry actual weight and consequences—the tension must be unbearable, and the pressures, and the fake smiles. I look at the people in the office and feel a pang of loss and gloom even though I know my gloom or pity is nothing to them. They are members of a herd that survives from day to day. When one of them drops, they pause a moment, then shoulder on. They hold high-powered jobs, or believe themselves to hold high-powered positions, at least that, but there's always another "executive" who's a little higher still, and fear is a constant, and the death mask hardens.

I want to sit here and write everything down, and I would do it now, but, of course, I have to rush out, the office is calling. Something's always calling, and, as the saying goes, c'est la vie!

A lazy day today. I got up late—10:30am—telling myself that even the commonest soldier is granted a furlough once in a while. And so I sat, reading and eating and taking care of small things, hand-washing my shirts, my underwear. Yesterday, I cooked dinner and Monsieur and I were absolutely delighted. It was a kind of disorderly and improvised vegetable stew, using my brain and everything I found in the fridge, and miraculously, success!

Today Monsieur drew my face, but he's not quite happy with the drawing, it doesn't capture me, he says, it needs more work. I shall enter the kitchen soon to prepare tonight's dinner, and then back to my journals, magazines, and books I want to read. When and how will I manage it all? Ponder, wonder, and keep the mind active. Needless to say, I didn't get any work done today, except for pensively contemplating the pile of typed pages on my desk. Will try again tomorrow.

These past few days, the weather has been gray and grim and gloomy—GGG. I'm sitting at my desk, Dinner is cooking in Kitchen, Monsieur typing away on his PC machine in Living Room, Music playing on the stereo. Fish tank cleaned today, food shopping done again, Breakfast and Lunch eaten, and Dinner cooking in Kitchen, as already said. John is coming tonight, to visit and share our dinner repast. What else? Read, read, read, drank coffee and smoked three cigarettes. What else? That's it. Moved around a lot, up and down, and here and there. Exercised a bit, trimmed my bangs, and made faces at the mirror.

Wouldn't you know that after four days of gray and grim, rain would join the triple Gs and turn everything wet. Even the Empire State Building turned black overnight, i.e., lightless. New York is falling apart, and Monsieur is on edge. Now he wants to go and live with John for two weeks to rediscover himself and us; in brief, he needs to be alone, which is fine with me, but he doesn't go. He brought it up a few nights ago, I said, Okay, but he hasn't left. Ever since I got back from my camping trip—didn't tell you about it, you were left behind at home, and when I came back I was plunged into Office Work and other Life annoyances and didn't find a moment to tell you about it, but, two weekends ago I went on a three-day camping trip to Fire Island with Lucy and her friend Emma, whom I had met only once before a few months ago when the three of us and Monsieur, too, went to dinner on the day Reagan was shot. I'm actually working on a story, wanting to capture the camping trip and its protagonists: Lucy and Emma and Reagan, and Monsieur and I.

Anyway, ever since I got back from the trip, Monsieur has been acting strange. I don't know if "suspicious" is the right word, but he looks at me as if I were a stranger, someone he doesn't trust, and/or someone he must guard himself from. This is kind of weird but is not new to me. Every now and then he plunges into states of deep resentment, like I've wronged him, or something. He becomes morose and "needy" but without admitting need or talking about it. Maybe he wants to feel, to hear, that I need him, I don't know. Strange man my Monsieur.

And so, he's been saying for a few days now that he wants to go live with his brother, maybe waiting for me to say, No, please don't go, I need you, but I can't make myself say something I don't feel. And last night he brought it up again, and I said, "Okay, if you need to go, go." This morning he said he'd be going sometime next week. We'll see. And, actually, I look forward to it: we'll be calling each other, he'll ask me out on dates, and we'll say goodnight at the door. No monkey business. And, being alone will help me to get back on track and work. Amen.

And, to close on a true and piercing note, here are the last two stanzas from W.S. Merwin's "Berryman":

> I had hardly begun to read
> I asked how can you ever be sure
> that what you write is really
> any good at all and he said you can't
>
> you can't you can never be sure
> you die without knowing
> whether anything you wrote was any good
> if you have to be sure don't write

It is 9pm and Monsieur, of course, is already in bed, sleeping like an angel, a drunken angel. Why am I putting up with this nonsense? Why should I? I shouldn't. I think I've stored enough pain and disappointment buildup in me. And I'm again in the frame of mind that tells me I'm better off on my own, let him leave already. When he's drunk—and he's been drinking heavily nearly every night for the longest time—he sleeps with one leg bent, his raised knee pulling up the covers into a tent, with him well-protected inside it and me outside it, and I wake up. Right now he's in his "tent" and I'm afraid it's going to be one of those sleepless nights when I have to fight for my share of the covers.

Am I going to go to bed tonight? I would like to, but the image of that knee and my beloved cover up in the air stops me. The farcical thing about such nights is that often, in the middle of the night, I kick his foot to bring the leg down and pull my share of the cover back to me, and he doesn't even know it, he never wakes. Then I fall asleep, until I wake up to kick his foot again, and so on. It seems that this is what I'll have to endure tonight, and my stomach turns at the absurdity of it, and the first thought that now comes to mind is: I don't want to spend my life with a drinker. The second thing that comes to mind is a question: Why does he drink so much?

Virginia Woolf in her diary when starting work on *Jacob's Room*: "Arrived at some idea of a new form for a new novel. Suppose one thing should open out of another ... The approach will be entirely different this time: no scaffolding; scarcely a brick to be seen ... What the unity shall be I have yet to discover."

Yesterday morning went to the emergency room at Beth Israel to get a tetanus shot—I cut myself at work the day before with an X-ACTO knife. They also took my blood pressure and I'm happy to report it's normal. I like the way my body functions. The doctor and nurse went into elaborate explanations as to what to do in case I have a reaction to the shot; so far, nothing. It was a bit sore last night because Monsieur, not realizing or not thinking about the shot, playfully banged my arm right at the site. Well.

And, finally, today or tomorrow he's going off to live with his brother, and I hope he finds what he's looking for. The truth is, I'm getting impatient with him, and this entire affair. Well, enough said.

I also bought a jump-rope and began jumping, one or two minutes as a start. Today I'll jump three minutes. And, we had a mini-blackout in a few spots in the city yesterday afternoon. Predictably, the TV people got excited and dramatized the whole thing, making comparisons and showing pictures of the '77 and '65 blackouts. Before they were done with their spiel, the blackout was over. I wonder if there was a blackout at all, or it was just their old-new habit to hype everything.

And now, Elizabeth Bishop on Marianne Moore, who lived with her mother on Cumberland Street in Brooklyn: "I never left Cumberland Street without feeling happier: uplifted, even inspired, determined to be good, to work harder, not to worry about what other people thought, never try to publish anything until I thought I'd done my best with it, no matter how many years it took—or never publish at all."

Last Thursday, Monsieur packed a few things and left on his long trek uptown to live with his brother where he wants to spend two weeks "to be by myself" and "to straighten my head out." I didn't see him leave—I was at work—but the night before he told me he'd be leaving in the morning. Fine. And this morning in the office, something strange happened: I was suddenly upset and all worked up about the stupidity and posturing involved, and worse, about him usurping/disturbing the routine/peace of mind I need for my work, and my life. I began to dislike him for muddying up my brain, and I still do, dislike him enormously, and I really don't want to see him anymore. I know I'm saying this out of anger, and I am angry, and my reasons are valid. I'm angry that he's imposing on me this masquerade of self-pity-indulgence. I have enough on my brain to worry about, I don't need his manufactured "problems," problems, it seems, he hopes to solve in a bar. Every time he called since he left, he called from a bar. Indeed, just the place to straighten one's head.

The good news is that I have bad thoughts only when I'm in the office, but here, at home and quiet, I'm calm again, working, making dinner, watching TV, reading in bed, and falling asleep enveloped in my duvet, and no danger of raised knees and "tents." And so, in effect, I'm the one who gets to be alone and quiet, establishing a new order in my head.

Monsieur called several times yesterday, wanting to talk, and after a couple of lengthy conversations, I'm not as angry with him as I was, and even invited him to come with us (Pia, Lucy, Emma, and Jamie) next Saturday night to a Simon & Garfunkel concert in the park. Last night, Lucy and Emma and I went out to dinner and drinks. It was cozy, and now and then I thought to myself, here I am, sitting and talking with friends, feeling free and relaxed, free of friction, free of conflict, no one is blaming the other for this or that, just sitting and talking about whatever comes to mind.

Monsieur was not mentioned. For now, I'm keeping our "separation" to myself, if only because I don't understand any of it and wouldn't know how to explain it. I have a feeling he's seeing someone else, or wants to be free to see someone else, or has met someone when I went on the camping trip to Fire Island and, feeling guilty about it, he has been kind of strange ever since. And, if any of the above is the case, what's there to talk about? This period may bring about a moment of anagnorisis for me, and I will welcome it.

And, life continues. Today we're going to a BBQ on Long Island—Lucy and Emma and I. I tell myself I should stay home and work, but I want to go out, I want to be with people, I want to be in a car and watch landscapes roll by, and then eat and drink in good and jolly company.

The cookout and the several hours we spent there turned out to be very gratifying, the food and company were good, the weather was good, the owner's dog was good, and the kids running around in the yard were good, too. We were there for the better part of the day and night, and I got home at 12:30am. I met a few friendly suburbanites—one of them, Peggy, a woman of about fifty, robust and strong—said she was never in the city and has no desire to visit it. All she knows about New York is from the paper. Even Brentwood has become too crowded and urban for her and she wants to move away, to the mountains. Instead of wasting time in front of the TV, she writes letters— about three-four an evening. She has forty-six pen pals.

There was also a black couple with their four kids, and after the kids were sent to bed, a discussion began regarding discrimination. Thomas believes that the situation, basically, hasn't improved much for blacks in the past 200 years, and that blacks should pick themselves up and start a revolution. Amen! Emma said, and we nodded. Then Emma said something that made a great impression on me, and, I think, on everyone else. She said that socialism grows upon the cesspool of capitalism, and that's where the young and the disenfranchised dwell. When the stench becomes toxic, it is time for revolution.

Thomas and his wife, Kendra, told us about the troubles they've been having with their neighbor; the police came, but did nothing. Even though I've heard it before—about threats against blacks who move to "white" neighborhoods—it was the first time I heard it from a black person, and the thought struck me that if I were born black in America, I would carry the weight of what whites have done and still perpetrate against my people, and there'll be no forgiveness in my heart. Kendra, Thomas said, was attacked in her own home, and there's nothing they can do. They say they may have to move away before it becomes too dangerous for them and the kids, even though the kids have it easier than the adults. It was sickening to sit there and feel helpless because brainless hotshots think that their white pimply skin privileges them to harass others.

A quick note before I run out, just to tell you that all's well, more than well. Since Monsieur has gone and the apartment is mineminemine, short stories, ideas, come at me with great speed, and I, like a dependable recording machine, write them all down, then continue to work on "Cinderella."

Here's a brief outline of a new story, so you know where my head is: a story about a woman who lets her lover read a story she is working on, a story about a woman who, in order to avoid conflicts, usually gives in and doesn't assert herself in her dealings with people, and soon the lover begins to treat her differently, it's a subtle change, she's not absolutely sure that he's treating her differently, and she wonders if she's the one who is now different, if she's the one who now looks at him differently, having let him read this particular story. This is it for now.

I met Monsieur last night and this time we got it straight: it is not a two-week thing—obvious, since nearly a month has already gone by. It's a limitless-time thing. It's called separation. Monsieur will look for an apartment. We'll meet once in a while. I'm to see other men, he's to see other women; the old, clichéd scenario, but I'm too "advanced" in brain-years to be willing to enter a cliché, or to repeat scenes from our past, and not such stellar scenes at that. My frame of mind is forming toward a gradual but definite separation, i.e., divorce. I think Monsieur knows it too, but, for some reason, cannot admit it to himself, or to me.

By now my close friends know it too. I only have to let my brain do the work, namely adjust to the new situation, while also seeking and finding succor outside myself, and tonight it is Sylvia Plath, writing in her Journal words I want to sing out loud: "For a time I was lulled in the arms of a blind optimism with breasts full of champagne and nipples made of caviar."

Plath—a kindred soul, and a full-grown genius at nineteen. Plath who says earlier in her Journal that she knows herself to be a victim of introspection, and yet, fascinated by the working mind of a lone person, she inevitably turns inward, "possessive about time alone."

Last night I had a momentary lapse, I suddenly felt— or thought I felt—a twinge of regret, of doubt, am I doing the right thing pushing Monsieur away instead of bringing him close. Then I pulled myself together—how? a miracle—and continued to read. Then I turned off the light and fell asleep. And slept well. And it's a bonus I cherish, having the bed all to my lonesome self, and if I want to read, no one is there to tell me the light bothers him. This is especially desirable now that winter is approaching, and in winter I like to read and write in bed at all hours.

And, I tell myself: instead of debating, tormenting myself with questions, trying to figure things out, let the matter rest, for now, wait and see how things develop. A decision in the matter can wait. Urgency not needed here, only plain, quiet living, work, and also fun and social activities. But, most important: concentrated work, which requires concentrated thinking, and deciding, and deciding again. The rest can be put aside, until it will clear away on its own, like a bad cold, an annoying cough.

A rainy day, and now, toward evening, the sun suddenly appears from under the clouds. The horizon between the buildings shimmers yellow, purple, pink. Einstein said that if we look deeply into nature, we'll understand everything. I look and understand nothing. Or maybe everything without knowing what everything is. But, the less I set my brain on speculation paths, the better. I have to be strong and keep in mind E. Graham Howe's sound advice: "It is better, if we can, to stand alone and to feel quite normal about our abnormality."

Fifty-seven warm degrees, cloudy, and a sun that has grown faint and has now disappeared altogether. We were promised rain, and it looks like we're going to get it. In the white sky, a large bird floats downward and I wonder if it's dying or simply tasting/testing gravity.

Empty head, making room for what I call Existential Issues/Deliberations, which bring about a general sense of uncertainty, of futility, all having to do, I think, with waking up with the residual debris of a dream that I can't bring up to the surface and which, I'm sure, was a disturbing one. Or, I'm also thinking, the dreams we can't "remember" don't have a story. They take us back to the primordial chaos, to the tohu va bohu in the womb before there were words or a story.

Today in the park, a middle-aged couple, somewhat odd-looking, sat down at the next bench and began playing cards on a folding table they brought with them, all the while talking in loud voices, oblivious of all others, the wife admonishing hubby regarding the laundry, or maybe she was not admonishing at all, that's the way they talk, and maybe they were not oblivious at all, but wanted to make their affairs public, wanted people to listen in on how well they manage. "We must do the laundry tomorrow," the wife announced. "Your turtlenecks and your shirts, the ones you wore once and put back in the closet. We have to get those ready tonight, so if I get up before you tomorrow I can start." The husband said it was an excellent idea and suggested they might as well also iron tomorrow, while the laundry is still a little damp when they take it out of the dryer. Wife agreed.

I shouldn't feel the way I do, but I do. It's 2am. Earlier, I knocked on Dorothy's door (she's my next-door neighbor) to ask for a cigarette and found her reading the Bible. She told me she reads it every night before going to bed. I felt so good and peaceful, soothed, in her company, and we sat for quite a while, discussing the Bible, Jews and Christians, modern life. I went in there cloudy and upset—I had called Monsieur and he wasn't at John's—but I felt calm and alert and revived with Dorothy. Now I'm sort of calm-upset because I called Monsieur again and he's still not home. Stupid me! I want to tell him we must stop this nonsense and file for a divorce, but something is not allowing me to do it, yet. But I will do it, soon. I don't like this half-and-half masquerade, I am tired of playing the role of the "understanding wife."

I wish I were stronger. I wish I didn't bother my head about where he is. But if this is the case—i.e., not caring—then why do I need this mess? If we have such deep problems, we should get a divorce and stop with the games. But I also know that I'm impetuous and, when upset, make decisions on the fly, especially now when I find myself thinking that he's spending time with a better understanding female, while it could very well be that he's spending time with a better understanding male.

I also know that if I had a lover, I wouldn't be thinking about what he does with his time. Does this make me a hypocrite? Am I lying to myself? Both? Or just confused and uncertain, looking for answers while the only logical answer is right before my eyes?

Many good things have happened since I last wrote. I went on another camping trip with Lucy and Emma— a well-deserved interlude, and just in time. They picked me up late Friday night/early Saturday morning—3am—we drove out to Lucy's house, went to bed for a few hours and at 10:30 Saturday morning we left. It was a bit cold in our tent at night, but the weather, on the whole, cooperated. We talked, laughed, ran, walked, danced, screamed for joy, did everything that felt good and liberating. And this morning I called in sick so I can catch up on my reading and work.

And here are notes and resolutions I jotted down over the past few days:

Another crossroad and I have to find my way. The only compass: myself. I also must begin to save money and plan my budget wisely. And I definitely have to put my weekends to better use and work. Fun with others has its place, but good, quiet work at my desk is deeply satisfying and its effects longer lasting.

I'm not very good when it comes to resolutions, but I have to learn to not anticipate this or that when other people are involved. I must let it happen. Whatever it is that has to happen.

I must not lament that I'm lonely. We're all lonely. And I must absolutely avoid thinking in terms of physical loneliness. I must keep in mind the many evenings and nights when I felt alone and miserable, with M. around. I'm perfectly capable of doing the same on my own, without the added burden of a sullen, remote person at my side.

I must relearn to enjoy my own company, and other people's company. I must discard nagging questions such as: why is it that lost souls fall in love with me, and vice versa?

And, one more thing, an order: Don't be so hard on yourself, Annette!

I need this shakeup to bring myself to a different stage. I've been plodding in the same morass for too long. I needed to wake up and I am waking up. I'm adjusting, gradually.

And here, to corroborate, is the last stanza from Sara Teasdale's "On the Sussex Downs"—

It was not you, though you were near,
    Though you were good to hear and see,
It was not earth, it was not heaven
    It was myself that sang in me.

End of notes. And, by the way: I've taken over M.'s desk. It's larger, and I prefer to sit here, in the living room—it's roomier—and write in you, little book, and work on my stories. "Cinderella," for now, is taking another rest period in a drawer.

Had a terrifying dream last night, worse than a nightmare: I was actually afraid for my life. Lying awake, I felt that a power stronger than me was trying to lift me toward and out the window. Never before was I so afraid.

I will tell the dream: I wake up from sleep because a power, or some kind of force/drive, is raising my lower body toward the ceiling. I'm sleeping on a bunk bed and, in a daze, I try to get off the bed and go to Dorothy to ask for help. My feet almost reach the floor but then, for a long while, I'm suspended again in midair, and then this "power" pulls me upward, my legs and lower body pulling toward the ceiling, as if levitating. Here I woke myself up, and forced myself to stay awake, my eyes heavy with sleep. I tried to rationalize the dream, explaining to myself the reasons:

1. the bunk bed because at Lucy's I slept on a narrow bed in a room she calls the loft—it's built to the side of the living room and half a floor above it;

2. coming back to a noisy city after a calm weekend;

3. feeling pressure/anxiety because my mother announced she's planning a trip to Canada—dates as yet undecided—and will stop here for a long visit;

4. because work (office) is upon me again.

And yet, while rationalizing, fear overtook me again as I became convinced that the power would win and I would throw my body out the window. I felt, still, that I was being drawn to the window, and I began to think that one night, while asleep, I might, like a somnambulist, rise from the bed and throw myself out the window, and people—my family!—would think it was suicide.

Awful thought. I almost called Pia who trains to be a psychologist. Then I fell asleep again and had another nightmare, this time about the office, feeling guilty that I called in sick. All in all, not a good night, and I think I must discuss this with someone, because, while awake, I thought I heard objects rattling on the dresser, as if a dybbuk was moving them, the same dybbuk that took hold of my body. I have to go to work now, more later.

6pm. Back from work, from a confused and confusing day. I forgot to mention that at some point last night I considered lowering myself from the bed onto the floor and then crawling to the living room, crawling so as not to be tempted to jump out the window.

I called M. during lunch and told him about my dream and he said he had the same experience a few times, it's the fear of losing control, he says, and, in a way, it does make sense, but something is still nagging at me, I feel it's too simple to dismiss the "levitation" experience and jumping out the window as fear of losing control. I also spoke with Pia, and we may meet tonight and discuss the Dream and also, hopefully, forget about the dream enough to talk about other things.

Every time I think of it, I feel that my dream has sexual connotations. I crave sex, good, loving sex, but do not take advantage of opportunities I have. When I meet men I find attractive, I act aloof and totally uninterested. Why? In some ways, I'm still the twelve-year-old who walked into a new school, into a classroom full of other twelve-year-old girls, a brand-new red bag hanging from her shoulder, her head held high and looking straight ahead, only to find out a few weeks later— already friends with the girls she had feared—that they had thought her haughty, with a shiny red bag to boot. And so, the question: Why can't I admit fear? Insecurity? Need?

11pm. Here I am again to say that sometimes, meeting people, meeting close friends, is the only true consolation. Spent the evening with Pia and we shared an easy-going and stimulating time together. We discussed the Dream, and her interpretation was that the dream has to do with something I need and want very much but am afraid to give in to it. She said it could be creativity and total commitment to it.

I keep thinking that whatever explanation we come up with, it was definitely sexual since it is the lower part of my body that is being pulled by this force, and jumping out the window may be fear of losing myself, even though it's kind of contradictory because jumping out the window is the ultimate loss. And maybe it's not creativity, like Pia said, but a relationship that I want and need, but am afraid to give in to it completely.

Everything passes. The good and the bad. I now feel somewhat revived and back to myself. I'm thinking that the dream was just an extreme manifestation of a deep anxiety I'm not yet equipped to deal with, anxiety about a fact I have yet to face. On some level I know that I'm at a crossroad, and that I'll have to face it alone. The good news is that I'm no longer afraid of it, maybe the dream was a kind of exorcism, maybe even purification, and that's why I now feel that the dream is behind me and is no longer urgent. And I do know that I enjoy Pia's company, I like to watch and listen to her, I like the way she moves and expresses herself. We decided to leave town and go somewhere two weekends from now and talk and talk and talk.

M. is fading more and more from my life. I'm more and more certain we'll eventually get a divorce. With our history hanging over my head, I can't talk freely and openly with him as I do with a friend. More often than not, I'm tense around him, afraid to say the wrong thing and trigger an explosion. Let me have a friend to talk to, and I'm happy. I want to be in the company of someone with whom I feel free to say whatever comes to my head, showing and revealing myself, my feelings. I don't want to feel constrained, having to calculate every move, every word.

Am I a lesbian at heart? No. If a man comes my way and he has the je ne sais quoi, I'll welcome him, but am not going to concentrate on pleasing, on "catching" him. I remember Tina, an older woman I met a number of years ago when we both worked in the same office, desk to desk, and who tried to explain to me the merits of marriage and marital bliss, telling me, in great detail, all the things she does for her husband, and I ventured once and asked, Why should a woman be doing all this for her husband? Her swift and firm reply was: "Because she benefits from it." Indeed, it may be a rational trading contract and a clever strategy, but not for me. I want spontaneity, from and on both sides, rather than contracts and rewards.

The mystery of my heart, if it is my heart. It could be any part of me, as every particle right now is pulsing in revolt against life, my life. I sit with you and stare at the still mostly virgin page, the straight, faint-blue lines that guide me across the page, and the faint-pink line of the margin that I often disobey. I sit and try, with your help, to put myself back together again, try to climb up from under myself, from under the cafard I woke up with, a heaviness, feeling tired and demoralized for no apparent reason, asking myself, why today?

And the sky doesn't help—low and burdened with clouds, like me. And a strong desire to go back to bed, but I won't. I'll stay here with you in the hope that by unburdening myself, my head/heart will clear.

Later. In the end, I did recover, slowly, cajoling myself with soothing words, remembering that nothing lasts, not the good, not the bad, and that this, too, shall pass, and then, reaching for Amiel, a small miracle; again words that broke through and brought relief, his words suggesting a way of life I'm already familiar with, having learned it from my father, and yet, it felt like something that had arrived just in time, something that I needed to be reminded of, and I instantly embraced it, feeling the words wash over me, while also wanting "always" to be added: "Since we cannot be happy [always], why give ourselves so much trouble? It is best to limit oneself to what is strictly necessary, to live austerely and by rule, to content oneself with a little, and to attach no value to anything but peace of conscience and sense of duty done."

And this brought to mind that, at times, when I sit with friends and listen to their stories, I suddenly wish my life were a bit more complicated, busier, more involved with people and activities, but, as I'm wishing it, I also recognize that such a wish is merely a "thought experiment" as Einstein would say, if about much weightier matters, because when I consider the headaches and confusions consuming precious time and energy, I decide I prefer my life to remain quiet and austere with a sense of duty well done, just as Amiel advises.

Night. 9:30pm. Days pass, and I live and learn. I've proved to myself something tonight: I can work after a day in the office. I finished typing one of my new stories and it still needs work, which is a good sign, it means something is there to work with. When I'm alone, completely alone, and no one is expected to come in and intrude, I can work at night. I only have to persist and, before I know it, it'll become routine.

And now a poem to welcome the night, "Women" by May Swenson:

Women   Or they
  should be   should be
    pedestals   little horses
      moving   those wooden
    pedestals   sweet
      moving   oldfashioned
        to the   painted

motions   rocking
of men   horses

the gladdest things in the toyroom

The   feelingly
pegs   and then
of their   unfeelingly
ears   To be
so familiar   joyfully
and dear   ridden
to the trusting   rockingly
fists   ridden until
To be chafed   the restored

egos dismount and the legs stride away

Immobile   willing
sweetlipped   to be set
sturdy   into motion
and smiling   Women
women   should be
should always   pedestals
be waiting   to men

Later. I'm more and more confirmed in my feeling
that I wouldn't want to have M. back when and if he
announces he's ready to come back. For the most part
I'm enjoying my newly found state, solitude. I even
"swoon" with the music of the word and what it
evokes. A small voice in me sneers: Are you sure? Or

are psyching yourself up for it? Time will tell. Whatever the end outcome, right now I know I don't want him back.

Interesting to note how the mind vacillates, restless-like, as it tries to decide what it wants, but I have to remember the basics, namely, that I have my work. We've played too many games, and it's time we called it quits.

12am. Poor Dorothy. She must be perplexed, or maybe not, maybe she knows exactly what's going on, but is discreet and doesn't ask embarrassing questions. She's about seventy, never married, possibly a virgin, and is always calm and accepting. She has beautiful skin and a wide smile—luminous—and therefore always surprising in its suddenness. I have yet to tell her about my new situation, but I can't. All she knows is that I knock on her door at strange hours and ask for a cigarette.

2am. I have difficulties with time, am or pm. I went to the bedroom, took off my wedding band and threw it in my miscellaneous drawer. I've come to a decision: I want a divorce. I'm not prepared to play his game. I am terminating it. Tonight. In my mind.

Edith Piaf is singing, Je ne regrette rien, and I feel the words vibrating in my temple, my throat, my heart.

Mon coeur qui bat, sings Piaf.

And yes, Annette is a little tipsy. The sloping script on the page, the wrung soul. Poor girl, what she's putting herself through. But she must admit she enjoys the music, she enjoys sitting here, late at night, with her glass of wine and cigarette. La vie de bohème. Like in the old days.

And that wedding ring: she never wanted to wear it, she doesn't like rings, or bracelets, or necklaces, she doesn't like the feel of metal on her skin, but hubby insisted she wear the ring, wouldn't even allow her to take it off at night before sleep, it hurt his feelings, he said, and she—the fool—obeyed!

We'll see what tomorrow/today brings.

3am. I'm still here, at my desk, with you, with my thoughts. I know I must gather myself and go to bed and then rise for work in a few hours, but it's hard, I want to sit here all night and wallow in my head.

Just to report that I finally did get myself to bed last night and arrived at work this morning more or less alive, but while sitting at my desk proofreading a report, I suddenly experienced a strange inner jolt and my whole being went limp, and I thought I was on the verge of a nervous meltdown, and then I recognized the symptoms I had experienced seven years ago when I first arrived in this country, it happened at the wedding reception of the son of family members I'd never met before, and where I found myself in a large banquet hall full of people I didn't know, when I was suddenly overwhelmed by an acute and powerful feeling of déjà vu, like I had been transported elsewhere, to another time and place, or, another place and time had been superimposed on the present scene, and I lost all sense of myself and dropped to the floor. I didn't faint, I don't think, but I did black out for a moment, and then became distantly aware that people were rushing to my side. I could have gotten up on my own, but I didn't, I let them help me off the floor and seat me in a chair and put a glass of water in my hand. A few minutes later I was fine, if still a bit shaken, and the evening continued as before. I was told at the time that it was a "panic attack," a term I had never heard before, and maybe indeed it was a panic attack.

And here is what happened this morning: while proofing, a sharp image of a man—I think it was a man—working at his desk came to me and it was *painful*—and this brought on a dim recollection of a dream I may have had in the night. I tried to recall the dream, or recognize the image and its origin, and then I felt this terrible sinking feeling of faintness and dizziness, like everything was draining out of me, I was being emptied of all content and substance. It was an overwhelming sensation of weightlessness, of nonexistence, of an overpowering apprehension about myself as a being, as a person, and I held onto the desk, knowing I must not stand up or call for help, so I sat there, waiting for whatever it was to pass. I don't know how long it lasted, a minute, maybe ten, and when I thought I would be safe on my feet, I slowly stood up and went to the bathroom to splash my face. I drank two glasses of water, and then walked over to Lucy's cubicle and sat with her, and she said it was a panic attack, and she also said, "Welcome to the club."

Earlier, browsing through an old notebook, I came upon this heaven-sent stanza from Letitia Elizabeth Landon's "Lines of Life":

Surely I was not born for this!
    I feel a loftier mood

Of generous impulse, high resolve,
Steal o'er my solitude!

If you were the nosey and possessive type, you'd open your mouth at me: "Hey, you, where have you been for the last few days? You have responsibilities, obligations, commitments, what makes you think you may disappear and ignore me like this?" But you're not nosey and definitely not possessive, but maybe a bit curious, so I'll just say: calm yourself. I went to Connecticut for a long-long weekend and had a most delightful and lazy time, and that's all I'm going to tell you. And it's not only because I don't really feel like writing/recording everything. I guess I would if I had sorrows to report and delve into. I'm too much in a euphoric state to sit and try to tell you more. Even my handwriting seems unfamiliar to me, and the letters come out screwy and odd looking, like I'm out of practice.

Forgive me, little book. I'm the same romantic and hopeful idiot that you must know by now. But I'm also mature enough to know that this elation won't last. More details some other time. For the time being, let's name him The Fling, and you can guess the rest.

And, I wanted to mention. Reading James Baldwin's *Giovanni's Room* last night before sleep, I came across: "I wanted to find myself. This is an interesting phrase, not current as far as I know in the language of any other people, which certainly does not mean what it says but betrays a nagging suspicion that something has been misplaced."

I should call M. and read this to him, but it won't help him, I don't think. He'll have to find it for himself, to come to whatever conclusion on his own. For now, he's still out there, apparently looking and not finding.

10:30pm. Am I behaving foolishly? I think I am. Yes, definitely I am. So many emotions run through me in every direction. I can't say/I don't know what name to call the state I'm in. And yes, it's that bad. It's a constant restlessness and confusion and anxiety over one thing or another. The reasons vary, but the feeling is the same. What is happening to me? I must recollect myself and become ME again. Was I ever ME? I don't know for sure, but I do think I was ME when I was living alone, years ago, typing away without fear, and with no à priori deliberation. I was hopeful, exuberant, spontaneous. In other words, young. Maybe I shouldn't listen to Verdi so much. Earlier, on her way home, Lucy dropped by for a few minutes, and I was calmed. I was glad to see her, to hug her. I don't feel this way about too many people.

I want to call The Fling again—I called him an hour ago, we had a "nice" quiet exchange, it was polite and general and went nowhere. I want to call him again and tell him I want more than that. I want to tell him that I think of him, but I can't do that. Men get funny when women get too demanding or "needy."

It could also be that it's not really The Fling who is the cause of this confused state, but rather the drinks

I've had tonight, and Verdi, and coming down from my euphoria. I don't want to work myself into a deep and hollow sadness again, but all signs point to the fact that I'm doing just that. And I shouldn't. It'll get me nowhere, and I need to avoid nowhere. I need to be somewhere.

Clever, clever Annette. She is not going to call anybody. She's going to hold her own on her own— yet another resolution. She's full of resolutions lately. She knows there are reasons for everything, and she's waiting to find out what they are and where she'll be led. She has yet to learn to control/hide her emotions. But, shit, she doesn't want to.

This is probably the first time she's used the word "shit" or the like in her journal, or even in general; curse words in English don't come easily or naturally to her.

Oh, my. I drink too much for my own good. Quite a statement. And my poor stomach. I have to learn to control myself. Too bad it has to be this way, but this is the way it is. I know that some, or most, people— "adults"—people like The Fling (who dubbed me a "truth seeker"), or even M., recoil from what they view as girlish demonstrative spontaneity, or an outburst of emotion. They regard people like me as too wild, too unpredictable, too impulsive, even foolish, and they retreat into their shells, judging such behavior as tactless and unbecoming. Lucy and Emma are the only people I know who welcome and embrace expressions of boundless joy and are only too happy to reciprocate in kind.

M. used to complain that I'm too excessive, too something or other. I expect too much, I don't act my age, I don't leave room for other people's moods and feelings. I listen only to my own voice. I spend too much time in my head and don't hear what others are trying to tell me. According to M.

Am I learning something about myself and the world? I don't know. Sometimes I think I do, sometimes I think I'm too stubborn. Limited. But I also think that essentially I'm good, and I do listen to people, I want to hear their stories, their ideas, I want to learn from them, and, besides, there's nothing wrong with sticking to my principles, my perceptions, or whatever it is I'm sticking to. It does me good, and sometimes not so good, but that's me. And I'm not special. Most people are also stubborn and they, too, have their views and tastes, but they have cooler heads and are better at polite veiling and eluding.

I now remember a night long ago, M. and I were not married but we were living together, he was sitting on the couch and I cross-legged on the floor, he was smoking a pipe then and I was listening as he talked and I watched him suck on his pipe and bite down on it. He was trying to convince me of something I could not accept, something at the core of my being, I don't remember now what it was, but to me, at the time, it was equivalent to him trying to bring me around to agreeing that the sun was the moon, namely, I had to agree with him that my way of perceiving reality was wrong, or worse, warped. It had to do with our relationship, with a fight we'd had earlier, and he suddenly stops sucking and biting on the pipe and gives me a look and asks/whines, with exasperation in his voice, why can't I admit that his version of events was the correct one, and I answered that he was basically asking me to lose my mind, and my answer shocked him, and surprised me in its clarity.

Thinking about it, I recall with wonder how the words flew out of my mouth, instinctively, like it was the only possible answer. Obviously, something happened inside me, in my brain, as I listened to him and digested what he was asking of me, and then the words came out with a stony conviction, but now I also have this image of M. and I locked in our brains, and not only M. and I. All of us, I think, are locked in our brains with our life experiences, and our basic ideas and perceptions about ourselves and the world, and when we feel that someone is trying to undermine the foundation of our being in the world, our self-preservation instincts kick in.

This is how the argument ended, and it now occurs to me that I could have thrown his whiny question back at him and asked why he can't accept my version/ perception of things, but, in retrospect, it would have made no difference. M., I now think, exercised argument for argument's sake, it was a kind of a verbal trick, a game, whereby he sought to establish his authority over me, over our relationship.

Rereading what I wrote I'm reminded of my first boyfriend urging me to come to his wave. Well, I didn't, and I won't. Let them come to my wave, and then I may agree to visit theirs as well.

I started out tonight thinking I won't write much, only a few words before calling it a night, and look what I've done. Suddenly, I actually feel content, on my own, listening to music, moving a bit with the music. And, basically, when alone, I'm free to be my sweet-bitter self. And yes, I do like myself. Right now my mind is clear, and at peace.

Happy morning. I woke up from a good, restful sleep, went through my shower and exercise routine, feeling one with myself and the universe, and now, slowly, getting ready for the day. But first the kitchen, and my banana and yogurt, and sitting down for a moment with the Book Review.

God! They just announced on the radio that Sadat was shot by soldiers during a military parade. He was shot with automatic weapons and was taken to hospital. His personal aide was killed. I have a terrible feeling that he's dead, too—automatic weapons!—and that this is the beginning of the end. The turmoil we've been witnessing in Iran will spread to Egypt. Lebanon and Syria are already involved in conflicts. The Middle East, more than ever, will be easy prey for Moscow and Washington who will battle over it by sending arms to "their" side, and the more arms, the merrier, at least for the arms manufacturers and dealers. And then what? Another war. I want to be wrong, but I fear I am not.

7pm. And, indeed, he is dead. My heart aches. The man I wrote to only a few short years ago for taking the initiative and going to Jerusalem to address the Knesset and talk peace. Such a man was shot by criminal fanatics too limited to grasp the consequences of what they have done. They were given guns and grenades and jumped out of a car fueled by ignorance and hate. During the day there was still a glimmer of hope that he was alive, as there was no confirmation that he had died. There were even reports that said he wasn't seriously hurt. I was praying for a miracle together with Hassan who is Egyptian and who works on my floor. But a miracle didn't happen this time, and the man is dead. I don't have too much passion for life right now. Everything seems to be falling apart and will continue so until we all sink. He didn't deserve to die like this.

Later. They were reviewing his life on the TV news, and it ended with Sadat's calm voice: "The body may perish, the soul will continue to live."

Yes, Sadat is dead, and I still can't believe it, even though I must. Everything is falling apart, my personal life, the world, and writing is hard for me because tears are flooding my cheeks. What am I living for? Why this awful feeling of doom and helplessness? I'm in bad shape right now, and I was in a fair mood until I saw Sadat's face on the evening news.

By the way, I succumbed again, I'm buying my own cigarettes (did I say? I quit smoking/buying cigs two weeks ago), and I smoke them. Not good, but I need them now, they do comfort me, they keep me company, as I write and listen to Verdi and sip my wine. It's all of a piece, inducing/encouraging myself to get back on track. The worst that may happen: I'll die young!

I've come back to myself, namely, I'm working again, steadily, and I feel restored, and brand-new. I'm completely myself when I am with myself. I listen to music—tonight it's been Verdi, George Benson, and now Brel. What a combo. Life feels richer, more meaningful, when I'm alone, and I've been alone a lot lately. I do all the things I used to do before I met and married M. Eyes shut, I lie on the carpet and listen to music without worrying about what he may be thinking about me doing such a foolish thing, lying on the floor, and asking himself: What is she up to now?

I give myself over to music, which, some would argue, is a "lonely" thing to do. I find—re-find—that living alone is my only option. And if I want to get high as I work and listen to music, that's fine, too. Time seems more consequential, fuller, richer, when I'm on my own.

On se retrouve seul, sings Jacques Brel.

What am I? I'm a good person, I know. At least, well-meaning.

Living alone is happiness tinged with melancholy. I'm content and melancholy.

People do get old, don't they? Old and wrinkled.

If we didn't have telephones, we wouldn't know we are alone. This instrument invites you to remember that it sits there, not ringing.

Sitting here brooding, I remember that people— M. is one—and even people who hardly know me, often exclaim: "You're naïve" or "You have a good heart." There was a time when both characterizations pleased me, I took them as compliments, but now, even when someone says it approvingly, I cringe inside, thinking that if we lived in a world where being naïve and goodhearted was considered the norm, such exclamations would be redundant, or, would not even exist in language, but in the world we actually live in, the people who tell me I'm naïve or goodhearted, are, in effect, telling me, wittingly or unwittingly, that they are smarter in the ways of the world than I am, or, worse, they tell me I'm a fool.

I'm having a French night. Mon père, mon père, mon père à moi, sings Gilbert Bécaud.

I went downstairs and got a slice of pizza with lots of garlic powder and brought it upstairs to be devoured. This is bachelorhood. I'm hungry, and that's a good sign. I'm also drinking my second glass of wine and smoking my fifth cigarette. Not good! But I want to sit here and ruminate, and I want to smoke, and I tell myself that I can't enjoy my cigarette without my wine, and that I can't enjoy my wine without my cigarette, and so effectively I damage my liver and my lungs and who knows what else, trapped as I am in the pleasure center of my brain, sitting here alone with my romantic notions of glorious solitude.

10pm. You're a funny girl, Annette. Where are you going, where is your head?

A gorgeous day out and, as I sit here, the afternoon sun on my face is soothing, and the radio in the background softens the air and cajoles. Last night Pia and I went to Fat Tuesday's jazz club to listen to Herbie Mann and his band. Later, after the show, when we sat upstairs at the bar, a man who had bought an album of Mann's music approached the bar and handed me the album, saying he wanted me to have it, and before I had a chance to say thank you, he left. Just like that. A total stranger!

Sitting here, it suddenly hits me that deep down inside I'm sad, maybe even very sad. Is sadness lodged in my DNA? I don't know. It could be my environment, what I see around me. Most people my age seem harried, hyperactive, everyone trying to look "stylish" and with the times, pushing for and pretending to be at the center of things, at the top of their game, they're blasé, they're on the move. And, of course, cool, a word I've come to dislike when misappropriated, when it's the new face on the old snob. A cool that stipulates you be haughty and cynical upon encountering the non-cool, or worse, the cool from a different clique who looks, at first blush, to be cooler than you.

The worst of it is that I, at times, feel compelled to put on the same aloof mask, pretending to have a great life because not having a great life means you're a failure, a whiner, in other words, a loser. The truth: we're confused and lost. Not all the time. We have our moments, but only when we open ourselves to another. So why do we try so hard to be cooler than cool?

I know I harbor fears and worries, all real, but also not quite real since they're in my head, as potentialities. If I'm a creator of anything, I'm the creator of my own anxieties, and it's probably true of most, we're Fear Machines, producers of anxieties and doubts. Often, when I wake in the night, instead of thinking good thoughts to put me back to sleep, my brain and I go racing from one corner of past misery/conflict to another, as if making sure that all my miseries are intact and nothing is missing. Sometime ago, at a lecture I attended with Lucy, the speaker said that if you have to talk to yourself and listen to the voice in your head, why not make it a friendly voice that tells you you're beautiful inside and out. Afterward, I tried to follow this friendly advice, but the voice in my head faltered and sounded false because I knew I was just following the instructions of a stranger. Besides, I felt ridiculous vis-à-vis myself, and this was the end of the experiment.

The speaker also said that one must not take to heart other people's stories because people always lie or invent, even when they believe that what they're saying is true; in short, we're all mythomanes. But, if we're all liars, wrapped up in our own myth-making, and since we're not supposed to listen to the voice in our head, unless it's a friendly voice, how are we to function? How can we even listen to others, while we suspect them of lying, and, at the same time, are also busy trying to negate our own voice, our story? And why should we ignore our own so-called lying/ made up stories if they inspire us when we tell them to ourselves or to others? And why shouldn't we trust people and the stories they tell us?

In the end, when it comes to human nature, such theories are yet another story, made of abstractions and guesswork and broad brushstrokes—interesting to listen to but hard, or impossible, to practice. Not to mention that nowadays the number of self-appointed gurus in search of disciples is growing, and, the more gurus the greater the competition, the noise, and confusion. Better listen to your own voice, your own intuitive story, and the stories of your friends.

Another beautiful day—the sun is out and bright, you'd think it was summer again, except for the chill in the air. Yesterday I was in bed all day, letting my gums rest, and finally done with periodontal work: had my last gum surgery yesterday morning.

And a strange coincidence just now. A minute ago I was marveling at the thought that since Sadat's death the sun has been out nearly every day, and as I was trying to figure out what made me make this connection between Sadat's death and the sun, the newscaster mentioned Israel and Egypt, and I began to pay attention and listen, and my heart stopped again, just as it did on the day Sadat was shot. Moshe Dayan died last night in hospital in a suburb of Tel Aviv. Heart attack.

Let the two of them—Dayan and Sadat—meet up wherever they are and try to do something for us down here. They've had a long shared history and their passing marks the end of a cycle: they both fought the British, they fought each other, and then the two of them worked toward bringing peace to the region. End of a cycle and end of an era.

Last night I was in bed, reading, when the phone rang. It was almost midnight, and I thought it was M., but it was The Fling. He remained on the line for a long time but didn't say much, maybe waiting for me to do the talking. I didn't have much to say either. I don't know why he called. I don't think he knows why he called. And, it is midnight again and soon to bed. And, talking of M. His phone calls annoy me more and more. He now lives in Brooklyn with friends. Who are the friends I don't know and don't care—I don't ask questions. I wish I had the courage to tell him his phone calls annoy me. I wish I had the courage to say: Let's call it quits. It's over. Let's get a divorce already. Ah, well. All in good time. But, I must tell you: Au fond, je suis triste, but mellowly so.

I want to say something, but I don't know how to begin. I want to be precise. In the past few months—after the initial two difficult weeks—I've been elated at times, and sad at times, but always—I can't find the word. Maybe, grounded. Grounded in the sense that deep down I know I'm on the right path. Even if it's the path of a single person, and "single" in our society sounds morbid. The truth: I enjoy having the apartment to myself, I enjoy the fact that I don't have to be home at a certain hour, worry about dinner, and, most of all, I enjoy being alone and being able to do what I want to do whenever and however I want to do it. And all this miraculously shows on my face and body. I look good, better than I've looked in years, and everyone is commenting on this.

Also, since M. left I've been sleeping well, having real restful nights, and my eyes and skin benefit—yet another reason why people compliment me on my looks. In a way, it is strange for me to say that I'm better and look better without M., and this after my years with him, especially when I think back to those moments during the first couple of years when, in spurts of spontaneous elation, I felt we would be together forever. Equally, I don't know if what I'm feeling now is a temporary exaltation of feeling liberated, or a lasting one. Time will tell. And, the Yankees won last night, predictably.

Woke up this morning feeling a bit something or other, but then, as soon as I walked out and saw people on the street, I was reconnected with myself. And now, on the radio, an interesting, if silly, historical tidbit: In 1917, when the US joined the war against Germany, American consumers boycotted sauerkraut, so food dealers sent a petition to the FDA, asking to change "sauerkraut" to "Liberty Cabbage" or "Pickled Vegetable" and so dissociate a solid staple from its German roots and restore it to respectability and market share.

Not too many blank pages left in this cahier, and soon I'll have to go to a stationery store and buy another. What began as an uncertainty (will I actually keep at it?) became a habit, and this notebook is filled with words, feelings, stories, historical events, and me. I like it. And here I am again, sitting down with a cigarette—shame on me—and listening to Verdi. Early this morning went to my periodontist who removed the dressing and took out the stitches. Thanks to him my gums are now healthy pink and, I almost want to say, attractive. I came home, took care of the laundry, had breakfast, and now will read for a while, and then sit down to do real work.

11pm. Work done, and then, sitting and drifting in my head, I found myself thinking again about this notebook, almost nostalgically—maybe this is my way of saying goodbye—and looked back to the time when I first started to write in it, and, for a moment, felt sorry for the girl I was, for what she had to go through, for what I had to go through. A notebook that began out of desperation and a need to vent, serving purely as a Sex and Squabbles outlet, and then, remarkably, it became much more than that, it became me on paper.

I wish I could add more sheets to it, instead of buying and starting a new one. I'll miss its density, its fullness, the physical sense of the accumulated moments packed in its pages, of times recorded and preserved. The thought of a brand-new book, like a fresh, clean start, doesn't feel right and doesn't appeal to me. I am loyal to things I've used and that have been with me for a while. I will come back to this book every so often and go through the entries and read and reread them. I enjoy flipping through the pages, catching a word here, a word there, my handwriting usually clear and orderly, but not always. The book is thick and feels good in my hand. The paper has been smoothed and softened by the writing. Laden with ink and words, the pages feel more substantial, weighty, and they make an appealing rustling sound when I turn them. And now to bed and read, a bit tired, but content.

Finally, the sun is out today after a few grim days. Yesterday, because of the dense, gray-white sky, I was tired all day, and even fell asleep on the couch, reading. But I did go out for my walk, and they were planting tulips in the park, to be buried under snow in winter and bloom in spring. And, in the tend-to-lazy way my mind sometimes works, I convinced myself last night that I'm allowed to watch the World Series—it comes around only once a year—and work all day today. So there, I watched the Yankees lose, and I have a contract with myself today: work all day. Will report results later.

7pm. Today was good as far as work goes. Typed a new draft for two stories and added a paragraph to a file I call "Notes." But now that the work is done and I sit here, looking at the typed pages, despondency descends. Tonight, for some reason, I don't enjoy my lonesomeness, but, as I'm writing these lines, I begin to feel better.

Those who say that writing is a lonely business aren't exactly right. We're all lonely, but writing, at times, shines a light on the lonely author bent over her desk. Still, writing also offers many moments of euphoria, especially when the work goes well. This is how I see it.

8:30pm. I'm reading over my Notes file and, without patting/flattering myself, let me say I think they're good. They ring true and exact, they feel authentic, by which I mean, they come from a real place, intuitive, and they light up my brain and pleasure it. I do feel, right now, that something basic is missing from my life. And I'm drinking my second glass of wine, one too many, as it goes against my resolution of one glass after dinner. I can't decide if I'm drinking because I'm sad, or if I'm sad because I'm drinking. Either/or, two facts are clear: I'm drinking and I'm sad. Now back to my Notes.

10pm. Worked on my Notes and now back here, with you. There's no one I can call and talk to right now, if simply because I don't want to impose my incoherent, needy self on anyone. I don't want others to feel sorry for me. I feel sorry for me, and that's enough.

Am I a lacking human being? A damaged one?

Years from now, when I read these pages and look back on this person sitting at her desk and writing these lines, will I be mystified by her? Angry at her blindness? Her helplessness? Or will I sympathize with her, ache with her? Will I understand the situation better than I understand it now?

I'm so tired, I can barely hold the pen.

The eternal cry: I'm good. Why do I suffer?

Just to report that I'm happy with the work I managed to do last night. What I'm not happy about is that last night I skipped dinner and drank instead. By 10pm I was—not exactly drunk-drunk but something like it. I felt faint, hungry, and totally drained and wrung. I brushed my teeth and put myself in bed so that I wouldn't have to make dinner and slept soundly till eight o'clock.

Back from an early-morning walk in the park, even though it's a cold, windy day. Had to get out of the house to combat feelings of failure and doom and end-of-the-road, so I bundled up and off I went and, watching the tired and grumpy faces of people going to work after the long Thanksgiving weekend, made me feel a little better—I wasn't alone in this, everyone, it seems, was feeling what I was feeling, we were all participating in a sort of communal commiseratory misery, having to rise again and schlep to work. Most days it's not so bad, it's tolerable, but sometimes your soul rebels and you want to give it all up, but quickly remind yourself that you're thinking Death, and you chide yourself, and you rise, and soon you're back in Life, seeing others on the streets, bundled up like you, and then someone smiles and says hello, and you smile back and say hello, a dog wags his tail in joyful greeting as his little face lights up when he notices you.

Thankfully, it doesn't take much to bring us back from the metaphysical brink. Still, the old year has become tiresome, day after day still trudging along, burdened down, heavily clad and winter-coated, so let it be over already and let a new fresh one begin. And now out again, to the office.

After a night with Emma, good Emma who saved my life, who restored my wellbeing with her straightforward, sober look on things. And soon to baby-sleep, I'm tired, and happy. Before Emma came I was a dry shell, hollowed out. Good night!

Laundry spinning in the dryer in the basement, and I'm up here, listening to the wind. The sun is struggling to come out from under the heavy white clouds, and I wish it succeeds. Earlier, people in the elevator, who had ventured outside, were happily/ excitedly complaining about the whipping winds and the bitter cold. "A Difficult Child"—a story about my sister and my little niece—is advancing slowly, but well, I do like it more and more. It's amazing how my confidence in my writing, in myself, fluctuates. Yom asal, yom basal. I have to learn patience and humility.

Later. Lucy and Emma are on their way here, and we'll be going to Becky's for dinner, where Lea will join us. I'm all dressed up, made up, after two concentrated days at my desk. And so, my dear book, this is your last page, your last lines, but, fear not, we shall meet again when I leaf/read through your pages every so often and re-live a few moments with you. Adieu!

Hello new book. You're Book Number Two. You're much skinnier than your predecessor, but it couldn't be helped, you're the only one I liked in the store. Book Number One is in the drawer. Book Number One began with Squabbles and No Sex, and you begin with no squabbles and no sex. The best state: you don't get the honey, but you're also spared the sting. Neutral. For now, what you need to know about me is that I'm usually stable and quiet, provided that no one bugs me. I may feel sad once in a while, but, for the most part, I'm fine with myself, especially when the outside world is relatively at peace and people aren't shooting or shouting at one another.

And, two pearls to welcome you:

Jorge Luis Borges: "All things have been given to us for a purpose, and an artist must feel this more intensely. All that happens to us, including our humiliations, our misfortunes, our embarrassments, all is given to us as raw material, as clay, so that we may shape our art."

Ursula K. Le Guin: "Even pain counts."

Yesterday I saw the most extraordinary film: the 1927 "Napoleon," four and a half hours of delight and wonderment, taking the imagination where it wants to go. It is fortunate that Abel Gance, who wrote, directed, and edited this masterpiece, has lived long enough—he passed away several weeks ago—to finally receive the honor and acknowledgment for his film that had been put away and forgotten six months after its release. And now, so many years later, thanks to a man named Kevin Brownlow, as well as Francis and Carmine Coppola, it's been brought back to life. It feeds you emotionally, intellectually, aesthetically, engulfing you with the love, the charm, the determination, and humanity of its creator. The acting doesn't feel like "acting" and every detail in this film is thoughtfully and tastefully placed. He made this film in two years, which is yet another feat of genius.

Aside from that: it is still gray and raining, it feels as though it has been raining forever. And, I joined a yoga class at the Y. I hope I don't find excuses not to go.

Later. Rain stopped, so went out for a walk in the park, marching under the trees and chanting: Thank you, God, for allowing me to have this life. An old man sat on a wet bench, smoking a cigar. A small squirrel stood on his hind legs, his paws at the ready to catch whatever the man may throw his way. Squirrels know from experience that a seated person in the park may have a nice crunchy peanut in their pocket.

On the stereo, Callas is singing her heart, and today is a Taking Care of Annette Day. Allowed myself to linger in bed until 9am, then got up, took a slow shower, and slowly began caring for my plants, dusting the leaves, picking the dead ones, and singsonging sweet nothings to them. And then, at the same slow pace, as if in a dance/trance, I began cleaning my bedroom—a thorough dusting and cleaning job, and then semi-thorough the rest of the apartment. Then I had a lavish breakfast and read until about 2pm. I do plan to get to my desk soon and go over my stories. I have a party to go to tonight, but I won't; I have no desire to see people and be sociable. I want to work and ride this newly found wave of self-sufficiency for as long as it lasts. I'm again—and I thank whoever is responsible—happy on my own. My pen and music is all I need. And food, and, alas, a few cigarettes. I'm smoking my third right this minute.

11pm. I'm happy to report that I did go over my four typed stories, I penciled in a number of good revisions, and then read out loud "Fat Chance," my first complete and ready to go story. I read it and suddenly tears came to my eyes as if I were reading someone else's story and not my own. I think it's well written and is honest, and that's why the tears came as sudden as they did; the last sentence did it. Which is what I want.

Best of all, I worked well today and I'm my happy-sad self again.

I'm taking a lunch break: had a soft-boiled egg with Italian bread and caviar spread. Now out for a walk, and to the Strand Bookstore to buy a present for Pia's birthday. I want to get her a book of Russian poetry. I don't know why my mind is set on Russian poetry. Russian—because she just came back from a trip to Russia and Mongolia. Poetry, I don't know. We've never discussed poetry—only prose—but I know she'll like it.

Later. 11pm. A most perfect day. Spent two hours breathing in the enveloping smell of old books at the Strand, which brought back the smell in my father's home, and bought a few books for myself and the book for Pia. I came home and had a message from Lucy. I called her, and we decided to meet for dinner sometime next week and then she'll stay over. After we hung up, I went back to my desk where work waited. Then dinner and a documentary about von Karajan on PBS.

I never had a desire to go to Austria, but now I want to get myself to Salzburg one day and go to the opera house, built according to Karajan's specifications and, acoustically, considered one of the best in the world.

I also listened and took to heart Karajan's motto: You have to concentrate on what you're doing at any given moment; when you eat, don't think of work, and vice versa. Concentrate on what you're doing and aspire to the utmost perfection. If you concentrate, it will happen. And now, before signing off: I wish I were surrounded by more people who create.

I'm sitting at my desk, naked, letting the sun do what it does best: warm me up. I'm working on a new story, and today is a day off for us, office slaves. This morning I read the paper, then went to the park for an hour. Everything sparkled in the park, every leaf, every branch, as the sun played light-and-shadow in the trees and on the ground—simply gorgeous and life-affirming. The calm, peaceful tallness of trees.

And now here, working. I've been in a strange mood these past few days, elated and sad at the same time. I think The Fling has something to do with it, not so much because I want to see him, but simply because I still try to figure out what it was all about. Ultimately, I guess, it doesn't matter, but right now it does. Well.

Last night I turned on Channel K—a new CBS cable—and caught the end of "Macbeth" with Ian McKellen. And when he gave the Tomorrow and Tomorrow speech, I was mesmerized. His eyes—and this is what's so great about TV or film, because in the theater, no matter how close you are to the stage, you can't really see it: the look in his eyes was the most disillusioned ever. Profoundly sad, mad, cold, nihilistic, and I'm still searching for a word that will contain it all—somber, sober. I guess disillusioned is the best, the most deeply and profoundly and nakedly disillusioned, darkly/gravely disillusioned, not momentarily, but for all time, the most disillusioned look I have ever witnessed and wish I never see in real life, it's so devastating. I want to find the speech and copy it down. We should have "Macbeth" in the house. Moment.

I couldn't find "Macbeth", but I did find the end of the speech in a book M. gave me long ago as a present, Asimov's *Guide to Shakespeare*:

"Life's but a walking shadow, a poor player
That struts and frets his hour upon the stage
And then is heard no more. It is a tale
Told by an idiot, full of sound and fury,
Signifying nothing."

Echoing Kohelet, it is beyond despair, and Ian McKellen personified it. Will now listen to Verdi's "Macbeth" while I work.

The sun is out again, and so am I, almost. I'm out of bed, out of the shower, out of the kitchen, and am sitting here with banana and yogurt. In forty-five minutes I'll be out the door, out the elevator, and out of the building and schlepping to the office. Last night I stopped working and went to see two films by Truffaut: "Le dernier metro" and "L'Argent de poche." He's such a good writer and director, so warm and intuitive, so funny and sad. Back home, before going to bed, I watched on Channel K a film by and about the dancer-choreographer Twyla Tharp. An amazing combination, mix, of classical movement—ballet—and modern themes to the music of Bruce Springsteen and Supertramp, themes of isolation, discord, separating and getting back together again, and separating again.

Lucy is sleeping in the bedroom, and Joe Papp is singing Hava Nagila in a silly commercial on the radio, promoting one of his projects, but still. Somebody, maybe a good friend, should tell him that if he must sing, he can join a synagogue and sing with the congregation. Yesterday afternoon Lucy came over, we hennaed our hair, ate, then went to meet Marianne, Lucy's friend. Beautiful, and immensely interesting. She's a published novelist and retired teacher—Lucy took writing workshops with her—and now works on a new, and also on an old, novel. She drinks and smokes, pot only! We sat and talked, and then she read to us chapters from her new novel. I was a little sleepy toward the end of the evening, but Marianne, much older than us, didn't seem tired at all, and, when we were leaving, she said she was going back to her desk to work. I looked at her with admiring eyes, telling myself that when I'm her age, I want to be exactly like her.

MARIA CALLAS. Tonight, on PBS, I happened to catch a great documentary about Maria Callas, narrated by none other than Zeffirelli. Maria Callas. What a name, what a voice, what a face. You feel the love, the pain, in her voice, especially in the high notes, and you're one with her in openness, in vulnerability. She was one of a kind. She carried the music, the opera, the entire orchestra, the audience. I'm glad she was (and is, probably forever) appreciated and loved by millions; it was the only real comfort she had, singing, and taking in the audience's response to her.

Again, I can't devote to you as much time as I want to. Again, lingered in bed until almost eight o'clock. The gray and cold outside did not encourage me to rise, inviting me instead to stay right where I was, in bed, half-listening to the music, the news, and the soft voice of the presenter on WNCN.

Not much going on except to say that yesterday, after yoga, I made myself a delicious dinner, including banana frites, and then watched an interesting program on PBS about public parks and plazas and how humans behave in them, what brings them to a certain park or plaza, and what keeps them away from another.

Looking forward to coming home tonight to the same program: dinner, and hopefully, some work, and then I want to watch Glenda Jackson in a new TV movie. And now out to the world, namely, to the office. And, it's going to rain today.

Welcome New Year, it's 4am, and you are exactly two days old. I woke up and thoughts began to roam and crowd in my head, so I knew that sleep was no longer possible, and I rose and came here to you, dear desk, and to you, little book. Outside, a few brilliant stars, and also a moon patrolling the sky. I like these small forays into the night/early morning. Now that I live alone, I can turn on the light and read and work at all hours. I spent New Year's at Lucy's party and we welcomed the future with cheers and fireworks. I stayed over and came home yesterday afternoon. Went to bed early, and woke up at 3:30am, tried to fall asleep again, but thoughts came and brain began to work, and, before rising, I thought about life, my life, about how I sometimes feel that life is a floating, that I float through life among people, I talk, I laugh, I participate, but am not fully there, am also somewhere else, deep in my head.

Maybe that's why humans have careers, marriages, kids, something that tethers them to reality, to others, to a community. And since nothing tethers me to others, it is my "fate" to be alone. I wasn't made for a "career" or "family life" and what usually keeps me afloat are my friends, working at my desk, listening in on my thoughts, reading the thoughts expressed by others in books and, lastly, coming to you, silent as you are, and always available.

Just now I opened Kohelet at random and "fell" upon: "For if a man lives many years, let him rejoice in them all, and let him remember the days of darkness, for they will be many; all that befalls him is vanity."

It is still dark out, but for me a new day begins, and hopefully not of darkness. Shower, breakfast, and all the rest.

My father used to drink and smoke at night, and that's what I do, drink and smoke at night: am now smoking my 10th and drinking my 4th or 5th glass of wine--not a full 8oz. but more like 4oz. I have to stop this because it slows me down. I have to stop this because I do it too often. The only saving grace: I'm still counting them, the cigarettes and the drinks. But, I also enjoy it, sitting here, quietly, writing or reading, relaxing, closing off, a pen in my right, a cigarette in my left, the glass of wine on the desk—one would say, a poised and tranquil queen. I enjoy it now, but it's in the morning, every morning, that I vow never to do it again, and here I am, again.

I'm not happy tonight. Not unhappy, but not happy, having watched a movie on TV rather than sit here and work, a sentimental movie that made me cry, "Blonde Venus" with Marlene Dietrich. Indeed, a blonde Venus, soft and pretty and feminine, all the things that I doubt I am. And so, if I'm none of the above, what am I? When it comes to sex, to the act itself,

I'm probably more like a man, or what a man is reputed to be, in the sense that I'm more of a taker than a giver, if only because I'm lazy.

More to the point, Work has become more important than Love. And I don't have love. I have love in me, but not physical love. I've had it in the past and will probably have it again, as long as it doesn't interfere with my life, with the way I want to live my life. I always want more than I have, but I don't want the routine of a relationship, day after day. The only routine I want is the routine of work, and for that I need to be quiet and alone, even if I have to endure moments of doubt, like now. Had I written something worthwhile today I wouldn't be in such a funky mood. And so, take a deep breath, Annette, and remember that you're in training. Be patient, your time will come. And, I do have my small fortress here: my desk, my music, this pen.

And! Before "Blonde Venus" I did start a short piece which I titled "Love Thyself." The opening is kind of sexual, and we'll see where it takes me. And, nothing is ever lost, even time, I will work tomorrow. Today is gone, but not as long as I sit here and follow the pen, watch it move.

News: I tore up the cigarettes I had in the house. One by one. NO MORE.

I also changed my breakfast: bought whole-grain cereal and now it's in the bowl together with the banana and yogurt and, indeed, tasty and supposedly healthy as well.

Since M. departed, I pay closer attention to myself, mainly because I have the mindset and the time to devote to it. I take almost an hour in the shower on weekends, and thirty minutes during the week when I have to go to work. And this is only showering and toweling. No primping, no make-up, no getting dressed, just washing and drying. What am I doing that takes so long? Pure indulgence under the stream of hot water while recalibrating for the day ahead.

8pm. It's funny. A few minutes ago I was sitting in the chair, reading, and all of a sudden I felt sad, and alone. While sitting there, trying to concentrate and keep on reading, out of nowhere and with no warning, tears came pouring down my cheeks, and I went to the bathroom to wash my face. And then I decided to go down and buy cigarettes, pour myself a drink and listen to music. I did all those things—put on a coat and was out the door—and here I am, sitting and writing, music is playing, and I feel much better.

Conclusions? Two. One: cigarettes keep me company. Simple. Physically I'm not dependent on them, but emotionally, right now, I feel I need them, and also a drink because I can't drink without smoking, and vice versa. Two: I got my period this morning and sometimes it does bring with it emotional upheaval. Therefore the tears, and the cigarettes. Tomorrow I may not need them, and I'll tear them up again, but tonight I need them. So I have them. Denying/depriving myself is not always the best and only solution.

I believe in yesterday, sing the Beatles.

In a dream last night I open my closet and to my horror I realize that it is full of dust and debris as if construction work has been done in my apartment. But no construction work has been done in my apartment, so God only knows how it got there, and how am I going to get rid of it, and who has the time and patience to deal with it. A very annoying and frustrating dream, and as real as everyday life when everything and everyone around you, including you, is infected with this modern disease, running around, trying to catch up with time, with errands, with work, with days of hyper-*hectivity*.

I called my mother this morning, and we had a good conversation. She was in high spirits, and it was easy to listen to her and to hear that everyone is well, and that my sister just announced that she is pregnant and is due in September. And so, just like that, another baby, another grandchild, another life. More happiness and sorrow, more light and darkness. And now I'm going to call her, and then work on "Men at Work" which is my next story to be finished and sent out.

Later. I've made so many mistakes in my life. Or have I? I don't really regret anything, so why do I think they were mistakes? Where would I be today if I'd made different decisions, or no decisions at all? Questions, questions, and I'll never have the answers. The only viable answer is that I did what I did because I had to, because that's who/what I am. I did what I felt was the right thing to do when I did it.

How do other people manage? Do they have so many questions, doubts? Another question mark.

There's no one I would want to talk to right now. And I have so many friends. The fact is that I become mute when I'm in a "mood"; I don't feel like philosophizing and commiserating and complaining about life. I feel heavy but am really empty.

And the people upstairs walk around all the time, and it sounds like they're wearing high heels. Where are they going? Nowhere. Just pacing around the room over on my head.

Let's hope this period teaches me something. At the very least, to not depend on anyone, and to not feel that I'm missing out on my life.

Tomorrow is a new day, and this is a new page.

Just now I asked God to do something, and then realized it is I who must do something. And I will. I can't go on like this, says Gogo, and Didi replies, That's what you think.

Stars, they come and go, sings Mel Tormé.

And martial law in Poland continues, and Lech Walesa and other Solidarity members are in prison. The world sucks, and I sit here, with my small problems—a joke!

So far, the new year is like the old, but I do have hopes for it, it is still young.

Got up a few minutes earlier than usual this morning—a small miracle. Last night watched "Rigoletto" on PBS. Louis Quilico—a name I must remember—was all emotion and depth as Rigoletto.

141

Pavarotti was the Duke. I sat on the floor, with earphones, immersed in the music and the words. Of course, I began to cry, almost from the start, especially when father and daughter sing their love for one another. I thought about my father who sang to me in so many ways, and I understood, once again, that I am what I am—my obsession with books, my frugality, my impatience with nonsense—thanks to him.

And I recalled the time years ago when I was invited to spend Passover in Chantilly with the family of one of my fellow students, and I brought with me the book I was reading at the time, Balzac's *Père Goriot*, about a father quietly suffering the ingratitude of his daughters, and, reading the book on the porch, sent me running to the bathroom where I sobbed for my father and his hard life. Eventually, I did come out of the bathroom and, during the Seder, I sang the songs I would have sung at home and told the celebrants all the stories connected with the holiday, stories I'd heard my father tell year after year.

My dear father. Mother.

Now, again! Back from the bathroom. What is it with me and bathrooms and tears? Too emotional, ma petite, too emotional.

Later. From the Kama Sutra:

"Three great aims of Hindu life:

Dharma - spiritual and moral duty

Artha - intellectual and material wealth

Kama - sensual pleasures

The man or woman who knows all three and acts with body, mind, and soul always here and now is happy through this world and the next."

Of the three, I have two. I still have to get more of the third, of which I have only half, or maybe two-thirds: my fantasies.

I just heard a terrible news story: a ten-year-old boy took a shotgun out of the closet, loaded it, and shot his babysitter. I should turn off the radio when they start with the news. All you hear is burglaries, rapes, murders, prisons, and then, cheerfully, sports and weather.

Now morning routine behind me—exercise and skipping rope—and am here with breakfast. I was in top form yesterday, industrious, and, in a fit of energy and determination, cleaned the house, did the laundry, and went food-shopping. This is doubly fortunate because today it is dreary out, rainy and windy, and since I was so good yesterday, I don't have to go out and can work all day. Everything I need is right here.

I am. Outside, the air is white with snowflakes—snow has been coming down hard since yesterday—absolutely magical. It is on nights like this that I feel like a true New Yorker, a real "tough" American who ventures out in the snow to see a movie—"Chariots of Fire." This is New York. You don't hide in your little apartment. You go out and smile at those who ventured out just like you. Violence is out of the question in the pure white snow. Everything is peaceful and still, and the parked cars, half buried in snow, seem like abandoned, crippled oddities.

I met Jamie tonight, we saw the movie—excellent—and then went to Bradley's. Until recently we used to favor The Cedar Tavern, but now it's Bradley's. At the bar, we had an interesting conversation with an older man, a published author (New Directions), who said that only two thousand people in the US read literary fiction.

And now I'm here, at my desk, with you and Piaf. And soon to bed and read until sleep claims me.

"Un toit pour s'aimer," sings Piaf.

Mimi is singing her sorrow on the radio, and I'm back home after a walking-and-window-shopping spree on the town all day yesterday and staying overnight at Pia's. We had breakfast in a coffee shop in her neighborhood, and suddenly Pia said, "You look beautiful this morning, your eyes." And it was such an amazing moment for me, the way she said it, spontaneously, I was overcome with a child's wonder, laced with gratitude. At Pia's, upon waking, splashing my face with water over the bathroom sink, I did look good in the mirror, thanks to the traces of my kohl pencil, smudged but still visible around the eyes, and my heavy white sweater with its high, round collar.

And soon out again to meet Lucy and Jamie, a plan that was originally an invitation to lunch and which I had turned down to give me time at my desk today, and now the revised plan is to have dinner. And so, not one word of writing all day yesterday, but I did compensate for it today, working a couple of hours on "Men at Work" if only to relieve my bad conscience. And yes, you're right, writing and socializing don't mix. I have to re-enter the magnetic field of discipline!

Midnight. This afternoon heard the Philharmonic in the rarefied company of women of leisure—a fundraiser—all of them, young and not so young, meticulously put together with hairdos and hats and sparkling jewels, and I, the pauper, masquerading in their midst, all thanks to Pia. When Pia invited me, I wanted to say no, but I said yes, I was curious, I wanted to watch the ladies, their mannerisms, their designer dresses; I wanted to hover among them, like a small, nearly invisible fly-spy. Nothing exciting to report, it was quite boring, yes, unfortunately boring, it seems that the ladies go to these charity events a few times a week, noblesse oblige, and they, too, seemed bored, but the cocktails and the exotic appetizers before the concert were tasty and tasteful and hit the spot. And, of course, the Philharmonic, the music, and the professional charmer Zubin Mehta, charming the ladies with light, uncomplicated jokes.

Afterward, we went to Pia's, she changed into "normal" clothes—I didn't have to change anything, I was wearing my best black pants and turtleneck—and then we went out again and saw a strange film I'm still chewing on, "My Dinner with Andre." Tomorrow will lock the door and work all day, re-starting, nearly from scratch, the draft of "Men" I've been working on. I'm not happy with it, something has gone wrong, am not sure what it is. Somehow, it seems that I've lost the clarity and focus of the story. I have to re-find it.

I also feel that I'm changing. I can't pinpoint the change because I'm in the midst of it, but I feel I'm evolving and becoming—a better human? Tonight I see hope, I see goodness, and I feel mellow. And so, goodnight to you, little book, I now have to leave you and go to bed.

11pm. Watched on PBS Zeffirelli's gorgeous production of "La Bohème" with Jose Carreras as robust Rodolfo, and my beloved Teresa Stratas as the delicate Mimi. During the intermission they showed a rehearsal and Zeffirelli actually crying when Mimi sings on her deathbed. I, of course, cried with him. One must cry listening to the purity of voice and heavenly melody. I should have been in opera, or at least backstage. In the interview, Zeffirelli misstated one thing: he said people don't appreciate/realize the physical effort of the singers. Wrong. People do realize and they show their appreciation in their applause, their tears, and their cries of exaltation.

Yesterday, while showering, images about my life in Paris came into my head, the public baths where I took my showers, not having one in my au pair room. Taking a bath was a luxury I enjoyed only when I went to see a friend who lived with an elderly couple. She was renting a room in their apartment, and when I visited her and

146

her "family" was out, I'd take a bath, or a shower, depending on how much time we had the apartment to ourselves. And then, the way the brain sometimes makes connections, the realization came to me that writing means organizing your thoughts and images, very much like you do in life, arranging/rearranging this and that on the counter, on your bookshelves, in your closets.

It's snowing out, and the sky is a white density and so are the sidewalks. This is going to be a fun winter with lots of snow, soft white snow. To conclude: I have to organize my thoughts, and I need to train my brain to focus harder and longer.

On the radio, a tribute to Thelonious Monk, who died a few days ago. Thelonious, what a magnificent name! I wish I could adopt it and start calling myself Thelonious. And, I'm finally alone and by myself again, the ideal situation in most cases. A hectic week, and this weekend, too, and therefore no words recorded here. Friday night Lucy, Emma, and Jamie came over. Emma cut my hair and trimmed Lucy's and Jamie's. Then Dorothy came in and we read a new poem that Lucy wrote. Then we read the new beginning of "Men at Work" and the consensus was that it was much better.

I motioned that we meet every other Friday and discuss our work. The motion was seconded, and a resolution was made. Then everyone left and Emma stayed the night, and also Saturday day and night. I love spending time with her, she's always fascinating to watch and to listen to. She works at NYU Medical Center and the doctor she works with has received a grant to do HIV research.

In the afternoon we went to see a mediocre play with Faye Dunaway "The Curse of an Aching Heart," and from there on to Sardi's—first time for me—and had a really good time. I expected the staff and patrons to be rather haughty and pompous, but I was wrong, they were friendly and happily talkative about the theater characters that frequent the bar, and we all bubbled along, with liquor and words. Later, at home, Emma and I continued the conversation and talked about health, beauty, sex, love, and, of course, laughed a lot. She left this morning and I was hoping to get to my desk and work but read and read instead. So, a full weekend and no actual work done. And, a recurrent thought: stop doubting/berating yourself. Work, and live.

Sitting quietly in my apartment, listening to a tenor on the radio—German opera. And the thought quietly comes that my "bad moods" as they were called in M.'s time, have disappeared. I wake up some mornings with a heavy heart, but it mostly has to do with existential worries, like: Can I survive on income from part-time jobs? Should I start thinking about a "career"? How long can one remain a part-time person, a part-time writer, a part-time employee? But these are fears, I'm sure, I share with most people: those of us who were born without a silver spoon. Those who were born with the spoon always worry about losing it, however long or short the pedigree. And those who have the top jobs always worry about losing them. Etc., etc. So in this, at least, in the worry-about-the-future department, I'm not alone.

Back from a night on the town with Jamie. No matter how often we meet, I'm always taken by her lightness, her spirit. I love to see her blush and watch her in action as she smiles sweetly—not saccharine—at a bartender, or anybody whose attention she's trying to attract. She says she can't help it, she's a born flirteuse. She keeps trying to teach me how to flirt, but I'm a bad student. She once dragged me to her beauty salon and insisted that I get a pedicure. "It makes your toes look like fingers," she said.

Do I want my toes to look like fingers? The question, idly, surfaced in my mind, but I let myself be led to the chair and got the first and, I'm sure, the last pedicure, because thanks to the treatment I discovered that my toes look much better when they're nice and calm and left to themselves, i.e., allowed to breathe, unpainted.

We tried to get tickets to see "Othello" on Broadway, no go, so we went to the Harvard Club where Jamie is a member and where she plays squash a couple of times a week. We had a long drink and off we went to Bradley's where we had a couple more. The only problem for me in a bar is that you're encouraged to drink. Another Jewish lawyer (The Fling was one) stuck to me at the bar. He was already drunk when he walked in and proceeded to lecture me about Jews and Germany. He gave me his business card.

Earlier, at the Harvard Club, a Russian émigré who's been living here seven years, took Jamie's phone number. I wonder how many cards and phone numbers are exchanged in the city every night, and how many phone calls are actually made. And now time to read a little and fall asleep. Tomorrow I plan to work all day and confront my evolving "Men at Work."

Finally got tickets and saw "Othello." It took me a while to get used to the bulk-heavy James Earl Jones— in voice and demeanor—and Christopher Plummer who reminded me sometimes of Ian McKellen in "Amadeus"—but the two of them did bring out the poetry. The sets were simple and absolutely magnificent, the basic feature being long, flowing curtains hung in different folds and compositions for different scenes. That's theater for you: a simple curtain can evoke menace, tenderness, be light and airy at times and, at others, heavy with foreboding.

And, I do amaze myself more and more. I hardly sleep these days, I get on average four-five hours of sleep, and yet I'm not tired. Energy continues to stir in veins, and in the brain. But I may be coming down with something, it's very cold out, and last night I woke up shivering in the middle of the night and put on heavy wool socks. And now I'll turn off the music, read in bed, and fall asleep to awake tomorrow.

No, not just yet. I feel like sitting here and listening a while longer to Van Morrison, smoke one more cigarette, have one more drink, and linger/drift in my head. Maybe a great revelation will come. One thing I know for sure: for now, I need my cigarette and my drink. I need a moment of nearly total relaxation, even if tomorrow I may be angry at myself and vow never to indulge again. I go with the moment, with the desire of the moment, and, in a way, this is good and necessary.

And, after having danced a little with Morrison, I'm seated again, ready for my séance with myself, the eternal trio, my cigarette, my drink, and me. Little book: this is it for you, and now good night.

I love Friday mornings when I go about my small domestic routines, breakfast, reading, laundry, and outside rain and snowflakes. I will stay here all day and look out the window, and, of course, work on "Men at Work." But first to the important task of waxing delicate hair off my legs.

And, need I say? Lately, I've turned into a socialite, if simply for the fact that friends say to me, Hey, do you want to do so and so and that and that, and I hesitate a moment, thinking of work, and say, Sure, why not. So, there I am, out on the streets of New York, going to concerts, plays, the opera, bars, but, in the end, I come home, alone. I want to hold someone, to be held by someone, and feel love, compassion, tenderness. I do feel it with my friends, my female friends, and I enjoy spending time with them, but I also need a little more. Ah, the fruitless but irresistible allure of the inaccessible.

Later. Dear Beethoven on the radio, and chicken in the oven. I forgot to eat today, and this after two days of gorging myself during which I suddenly developed this urge for scallions, I smelled them everywhere, and consumed them whenever I could, to the point where I feared that I might be pregnant, which would have been some kind of miracle and a news-making event, namely, another immaculate conception.

And so, today no food, but will eat later at the party I decided to go to after all; the chicken will be eaten tomorrow. Earlier, at the typewriter, I typed two sentences that came at me out of nowhere: "In the background there's a sad face. I don't know who it belongs to, but it's there, in its rightful place."

Last night I saw John Guare's "Lydie Breeze," directed by Louis Malle—Malle's first theater work. If these two names were not connected with the production, I would have easily concluded it's a confused play that tries to do too much and fails. But since these names are connected with the play, I began to wonder if I missed something, but, in the end, I conclude again it was an exercise in futility, people moving and talking on stage, but "dead" and removed, never reaching or touching the audience. It could have worked better as a film where they wouldn't be talking about what happened but would make it happen.

Most of the action consists of the characters recounting events they all know about, which means they are rehashing the facts for the audience's benefit, and the entire play is exposition. If the story and the actors had been compelling, then at least it would have been worthwhile to listen and pay attention. But, as it stands, it involves the tired old story of a man shooting and killing his best friend because the friend betrayed him with his wife and gave her syphilis to boot, which she, in turn, gave to the son of her lover the day her husband shot her lover. The son "reappears" after many years to avenge his father and to kill the wife who gave him the disease, but the wife had committed suicide years before, and the husband became an alcoholic after he was released from prison, and the son learns that he has given the disease to the maid, and the two of them commit suicide by going into the sea—to be cleansed?

It could have worked if it were directed and acted as a comedy of the absurd, and, if the way I tell it sounds convoluted, it is, and worse, the story is messy with too many entangled and dangling details, and the retelling is nearly robotic. Too bad. Now that I have written my critique of it, it's time to stop and go about the business of the day.

Later. Midnight. What a good and eventful day. Read all morning, went for a job interview—decided I need to find a fulltime job—came home, had lunch, worked a few hours, and then out again to see two films: "Why Would I Lie?" a sweet and warm film, and "The French Lieutenant's Woman," adapted by Pinter from Fowles's novel. The dialogue and actors were, as expected, excellent, but the real jewel was Meryl Streep. I love to watch her. I love to watch what she does with her face. And even though you know you're looking at Meryl Streep, you don't see her, you see the character she is playing.

And now here, and off to bed and finish the day with the wonderful, intriguing stories of Barry Hannah. Good night!

I feel that, as of late, this cahier has become a sort of fact-reporting depository. Again I feel that I keep my thoughts to myself instead of putting them on paper. A convenient excuse would be that nothing of "importance" or, nothing clear, surfaces when I sit down to write here. Another excuse: I'm always in a hurry and don't devote enough thinking time when I come to you. But, at least, when I come here I enjoy a sit-down with you, however brief, a sit-down with myself, putting myself on the page, writing and talking to both of us and listening to myself as I write myself, and possibly also listening to silent you.

And, I do have good news to report: I did manage to finish a draft of "Men at Work," and even began a new draft, and so, some things are moving, including rejection slips in the mail. Friends who read my stories like them, but magazine editors have a different agenda, different criteria, they want what they call a "handle," they want a "plot." Am I to strive for a plot, force a plot on my stories, or keep doing what I'm doing? The latter, probably, especially since my idea of "plot" is different from theirs, not to mention sensibilities. And so, in the meantime, I'll continue to have my doubts and momentary uplifts, until acknowledgment knocks on the door. Ah, well, no use complaining, keep doing what I'm doing without expecting immediate results.

This is one of those quiet evenings when I feel somewhat alone to myself. I know I have friends out there, but... I guess this restless feeling started this morning after that interview with the office manager at Harcourt Brace Jovanovich. As to be expected, the salary is ridiculously low—at the most $250 a week. These employers expect you to be a junior genius for no money. Well, I may still decide to see the VP himself on Thursday for the scheduled second interview, but it's 99% out of the question. Now out for my yoga class!

11pm. Had a rejuvenating yoga class, went through the Help Wanted section, and I'm finishing off the day with cigarette number four and a drink of vodka & grapefruit juice & lots of crunchy ice cubes I like to chew on. Good night.

3:30am. Yes, it is that ghostly hour again, and I'm back from a night on the town. La vie de bohème—it's good as long as it lasts and, afterward, gray sediment. Ah, well.

But, let's not see everything in gray. I did work today and finished a new—final?—draft of "Men at Work." It may still need more revisions, but it is basically done, and I like it. In the evening, Lea came over for dinner and then on to Broadway to see "Crimes of the Heart" by Beth Henley, good dialogue and overall construction—she doesn't leave loose ends. One of the actresses, Mia Dillon, was perfect, mainly using her voice to convey emotions. After the play, Lea wanted to go home, so we parted, she uptown, moi downtown, and, not done with the night, called Jamie from a phone booth, and off we went to Bradley's...

And, as I'm writing, I feel that something good is going to happen to me, and soon, and I'm going to make it happen.

And I must stop being indifferent and/or hesitant about flirting and men, says Jamie. I try to explain that I'm not really into it, I'm not comfortable flirting, and when I meet someone I think I may like, I clam up, but she won't hear of it. And so, from now on I must remember that a positive frame of mind and aggressive action are the needed ingredients. It is all a game and I'm going to try and learn and maybe follow the rules.

Where have I been these past few days? Running around to employment agencies—an awful experience, not to be repeated. On the positive side: changed the ending of "Men," a minor change but significantly for the better, and will be sending it out today. Have been meeting people and friends, it was all good and exciting, until this morning when I became anxious about neglecting my work, but now am composed again.

Also, since Monday I've been smoking a lot and therefore the anxiety and a heart that's beating too fast. I'd better calm and slow down. Will look over the paper in search of a job, custom-made for me, and then will get myself to the office. And tonight, I vow, will be a quiet one at home. This week has been much too hectic and rushed, but the positive thing is: all my friends are keeping their ears open on my behalf, so it's a matter of time before I find fulltime employment. No need to panic and/or rush things. I think that the craziness of the past few days, and especially the typing tests (!) at the employment agencies, bred anxiety and bitterness—they see a female, and before saying a word or asking any questions they lead her to a typewriter, and she, the sheep, follows. Interesting: as I was thinking "typewriter" and began to write the word, I was thinking: guillotine.

It's funny. I opened the book, saw the drawing/doodle on the reverse side of this page, and a dream from last night came vividly to me for a short spell, and I remembered that in the dream I made a large abstract painting, rich in color, and in the dream I am surprised because I know that technically speaking I don't handle color too well. There was more to the dream, but that's what I remember.

Yesterday I was tired almost the entire day and went to bed early. Also, went for another job interview, this time at a small film company. The producer, a young guy clad in a three-piece suit, was hanging back in his swivel chair, his ankles comfily crossed on his desk (i.e., in my face), a big, fat cigar protruding from his mouth. He was somewhat arrogant but also a bit shy, not yet complete and at ease with the image he was trying to project.

Probably a recent success and it does take getting used to. And now to story business.

Last night something wonderful happened. Jamie and I were on our way uptown to catch a movie, when I said: Let's see if we can get tickets to the opera. And we did. It was 7:30pm and we walked up to the box office and got two standing-room tickets for "Il Trovatore." I think New York is the only place in the world where you can do that. And if we couldn't get tickets at the Met, we could have walked over to the City Opera box office and get tickets for "Madame Butterfly."

The production elements were so-so, but, as usual, it is the music and the singing that matter most. Toward the end of the fourth and last act, the heel of my left boot gave in and broke and I had to limp the rest of the evening, which ended "somehow" at Bradley's, with me and Jamie a bit tipsy and giggly and gay like two birds welcoming spring.

And this morning the sun is out and it's warm and I may go out later for a walk, and then back to "Vaseline"—started a new version, as well as a new opening for "Technicolor," and I like it better.

And here, the last lines of David Ignatow's "Against the Evidence":

I stroke my desk,
its wood so smooth, so patient and still.
I set a typewriter on its surface

and begin to type
to tell myself my troubles.
Against the evidence, I live by choice.

It is gray again, and the same forecast for tomorrow.
On the radio, Mel Gussow is talking about the
wrecking ball that brought down the Morosco
Theater. And this despite the demonstrations, the
court appeals, and the general outcry. It is rubble now,
like the Bijou Theater, and more demolitions are in the
offing. The heart aches. I keep thinking about what
goes on in the mind of the person who sits tall in his
destroyer machine, pushes a button, and an old
landmark sinks and then cleared away like any debris.
Not to mention the bureaucrat who signs the order.

Yesterday, I finished the second draft of "Vaseline,"
and this weekend I plan to retype a third and possibly
final draft. I decided not to linger so much on each
story—"Men at Work" and "Fat Chance" went through
at least ten drafts each—but try and demand more of
myself in focus and deliberation right from the start.
Finish the stories and send them out.

Last night watched the academy awards and was
happily surprised: well produced and a spectacle to
watch. John Carson finally eased into his role and was
funny and relaxed. A special award went to Barbara
Stanwyck, who was very moving in her acceptance

speech, addressing William Holden, wherever he may be: "Golden boy, you finally got your wish." He had always wanted her to get it, and she never did, which is amazing when you look back on her long career, and we did look back last night on the screen, watching her in all the different roles she played, her intelligent lively face, eyes, smile.

And so, last night she finally received it, but he—Holden—had gone the way of every mortal. Still, he may have watched the proceedings from wherever he is. Danny Kay received a special award for his work with UNISEF. Katharine Hepburn won best actress, Henry Fonda, best actor, the great John Gielgud best supporting actor—but, unfortunately for us, the three of them were not there to receive it personally—and Maureen Stapleton for best supporting actress in "Reds." Warren Beatty best director, and "Chariots of Fire" best film, best music, best costumes—right down the line the same choices I would have made, except for adaptation to the screen: I would have chosen Pinter for "French Lieutenant" instead of Thomson who got it for "Golden Pond." Bette Midler was up there to bestow an award, and she stole the show. I think this is the first time I actually enjoyed the ceremony. And now to work.

It's hard to believe but April is here. This winter indeed went by in a flash. And today is a real day of spring, and so I'll go to the park and, later on, I'll go out again and take a long walk. The plants watered, the laundry spinning downstairs, and I, too, am watered and spinning, and this brings to mind that this week, too, zoomed past—I could have sworn that I'd watered the plants a couple of days ago—I water them once a week, on Saturday. At any rate, I had a productive week: "Vaseline" and "A Smile" under the belt and tomorrow I'll retype "Vaseline."

Later. And here I am again, late at night, after a good day's work, with my last cigarette and drink. Earlier, in the park: a toddler, a large leaf in his hand, chasing after a pigeon. And soon to bed, to my book, to my soft covers, then time to close my tired eyes and sleep. And tomorrow morning wake up to sun and music and work, and then Monday, and out to the real world, to my $-making job.

In a way, if I do find a fulltime job, I'll be a little sorry to leave the law firm. Some of the people are nice, even funny, and Sheila, ever since that last incident, leaves me alone and no longer dares bug me. I don't remember if I reported this here, but, briefly, she got on my case again a couple of weeks ago, and I listened to her rant, and then stood up, said I didn't feel well and left, thinking I'd never come back, but, on the way home, polite and gentle people going past on the street reminded me that Sheila was only one person, and that there was a world of people outside the narrow confines of the office, and that all offices are one office in the sense that the system is the same everywhere, and I did go back a day later and, as said, peace everlasting between me and her.

I still believe that all offices are the same and that I might as well stay with the familiar, but now I also think that I need more cash, unless I keep my expenses to a minimum.

Reading Friedrich Percyval Reck-Malleczewen's amazing diary (what a name! a Prussian aristocrat), and the way he talks about Germany in the late thirties/early forties is disturbingly familiar. It feels as though he's talking about us, today. "What else can be the meaning of this pervasive feeling of total bankruptcy, this secret fear and trembling like the feeling that precedes a great storm, of these spiritually empty people? We live in a gigantic spiritual vacuum. At any moment, awareness of the vacuum, and of the horrifying chaos, could bring cataclysm."

He talks about Mass Man who "moves, robotlike, from digestion to sleeping with his peroxide-blonde females, and produces children to keep the termite heap in continued operation... A whole people drunk on the success of a series of political robberies, thundering approval in the movies when the newsreel pictured burning men: a bloodthirsty mob roaring rapturously at the sight of human torches plummeting out of exploding tanks. There they all are before my eyes: beer-soaked old pinochle players dividing up continents over their steins."

It is heart-wrenching to read and try to imagine his grief, his pain, living among people who, seemingly overnight, have become blood-thirsty beasts, drunk with their misguided idea of glory. And yet, it is also strangely uplifting to read as proof that no matter how oppressive and power-obsessed the regime, there will always be those who will oppose evil, despite the danger to themselves. Reck-Malleczewen died in Dachau in 1945.

Winter weather is back, it is cold and breezy, and we had snow yesterday, a snow storm at that, a blizzard gift in April. It's all ice out there, and it snowed again today. This year, so they said on the radio, is the first time in record-keeping history that it snowed in April.

And, something has changed in my body as well, or is it simply the change of season? For the past few days I've been waking up around 5am, floating between sleep and wakefulness till 7am. It's as if my body tells me I only need six hours of sleep.

Today I want to work some more on "A Smile," and devote more thinking- time to "Vaseline," and, finally, also do my yoga exercises on the carpet since I won't be going to yoga class. And tonight, if I decide I can afford it, I'll see Beethoven's "Il Fidelio"—standing room, of course. Sometimes I find it hard being shut in all day because I start to worry about money, or worse, I begin to doubt my existence.

And, while worrying about such trivialities, I read a review of *The Fate of the Earth* by Jonathan Schell about the real possibility of a nuclear war that will annihilate us all, including me and my petty thoughts about employment, me and my stories, and you, little book, we will all be incinerated, and no more worries, no more operas, just complete and lasting silence.

And, à propos, and directly from the radio: there's a new idea in the world and they call it "eternal inflation," an inflation that has nothing to do with economics, but with the cosmos and the Big Bang, and it basically says that the universe will continue to expand forever. Well, maybe our forever is not quite eternal, and maybe as the cosmos continues to expand it will impact gravity on our planet, and earth and life "as we know it" will be hurled into a gigantic cosmic whirlpool. Voilà! My thought for the day.

Yesterday came and went with me bent over my desk, stopping only for bodily demands—food and bathroom. I worked mostly on "A Smile," advancing slowly, with the quiet confidence that is now the companion of habit, routine, and devotion. And today, so far, has been a good and slow and focused day, albeit differently. Haven't felt this happy-tired in a long while, physically as well as mentally, no energy to work or do anything that spells work, and so read all morning, dozing off for short stretches on the couch, interrupted by phone calls.

And now—2pm—down for a walk and will probably have pizza for lunch. Or a bagel and cream cheese. I'm so out of it, I don't even feel like preparing something to eat. Strange.

Tonight to Jamie for dinner and I hope that by evening I'll be awake and social.

April is almost over, and a wintery one it sure was, and today, as April departs, it is still cold, windy, and rainy, and Britain and Argentina warring over the Falkland Islands, this whole affair is so absurd, and in my naïve silly thinking I say to myself that such human follies do not belong in the twentieth century, but obviously they do. People clamor for action to relieve the monotony of their lives, and their so-called leaders comply, they press the "mass entertainment" button and the noise begins.

And yesterday I fell in the street and have a nasty cut on my leg. I am calm and composed about it now, but yesterday I cried, but also laughed with Pia who was with me to witness it, I was crying and laughing because it did give me a jolt and a shock to slip so extravagantly and land on the wet pavement, and then to realize that I was bleeding. Then the bleeding stopped, and I was fine. Pia took the subway, and, as I walked home, I started bleeding again, and when I finally arrived here, alone and bleeding, I was crying again, this time uncontrollably, and only after I went into Dorothy's, who served as a nurse during World War Two, and she reassured me it was nothing serious, the crying stopped. I am definitely, at times, a little baby, or an overly emotional adult.

Still and quiet and dark night-sky in the window, but we did have two days of real spring weather, warm sunshine, at least that. My mother is here for a ten-day visit, and, of course, we had a fight as soon as she arrived. She brings out the worst in me, or I bring out the worst in me when she is present. But tomorrow I'll definitely do my utmost to ignore the remarks that annoy me, or the way she looks at me sometimes when she tries to figure out something I don't want to talk about, namely, M. But, ultimately, I think the underlying problem is that she brings back memories of bitter acrimony that I try to suppress but can't stop them from agitating right under my thin skin.

I now solemnly swear, and for the last time, that I will try to appreciate her the way she is. What I think is happening between the two of us is that I expect her to complain about one thing or another, and am therefore cold and guarded with her, defensive and impatient and "somber," not allowing her the slightest opening to voice whatever it is she wants to say, if anything. I must stop this and be nice to her, be open and loving, show her a good time. I must. For my own sake, if not for hers, because I know that one day it will come back to haunt me. I must be patient.

I find myself wondering—and sometimes answering in the affirmative—if indeed I am a terrible person. And it is too easy to compare myself to her and to blame her for the similarities I find and don't like, as, for instance, the way she is in the morning, subdued, sitting with her coffee and cigarette, her face sour with sleep. M. used to complain about me, about the way I act in the morning. But I also think that she is this way because of the way I treat her. She is guarded with me the way I am guarded with her, the way I was guarded with M., if for different reasons. And so, whatever the case, I must make an extra effort and try harder to be nice and patient and open and loving with MY MOTHER!

In my defense: I know I'm not the perfect welcoming hostess, especially with guests who stay longer than one or two nights, they disrupt my routine and, in her case, take my bed and effectively chase me out of my bedroom. This is not a complaint, but simply a statement of fact. And I'm exhausted. I don't get too much sleep and the sleep I do get is restless because the living room couch is uncomfortable. I'm not equipped to take care of and deal with guests. But, enough with the bad! Tomorrow is a new day.

Today Mother and Daughter were good girls. Reconciled. Mother is a bit under the weather, and I got my period this afternoon, which may explain my short temper these past two days. I came back from work an hour ago, and despite my fatigue scrubbed the bathtub and prepared a hot foamy lavender bath for her, and dinner is cooking on the stove. I'm a good girl again, but too tired to write.

Mother and daughter had a heart-to-heart talk, and I am super glad for it. Now, face to face, she wanted to know more about the "situation" and, noticing my reluctance, she was patient and considerate, didn't ask about the how and the why and simply advised me to end it, saying that this in-between, unresolved situation is unhealthy for me, and that I must decide one way or the other, instead of needlessly prolonging it, and I agreed and said that I'm getting there, which is the truth.

And she is right: no use prolonging it much longer—cut it. And, of course, M. and I can remain friends, whatever it means in our case. My mother is not friends with my father, she cut it, and that was that. They don't see or talk to each other, unless there's a wedding or a funeral.

The better news is that we are getting along, possibly better than at any time in the past that I can remember, and, right now, I feel love for her. She is not "pushy" for "pushy" sake (actually, she's not pushy at all, she's quite restrained and even timid), but she is anxious for me and she worries and doesn't want me to suffer. This is a funny thing about parents, always wanting to protect their child, no matter how old the child is, no matter that the parents themselves suffered and still suffer, like everyone else, but the child, the child must not suffer.

And a funny, sweet thing: earlier, on the subway, an older man smiled at her before he got off. He had been sitting across from us and I noticed him watching her, and I happened to be looking at her when she realized that he was watching her. She averted her eyes, like a schoolgirl, and then sneaked a glance at him to ascertain that yes, indeed, he was watching her. Ah, romance. We all want it, no matter how advanced in age, we are flattered and pleased when someone pays attention to us, we the mortals, immortal in our feelings, fears, wants.

After an absence of a couple of days, here I am again, lying in my improvised bed in the living room, gazing at my goldfish and thinking of all the things I have to do today. And here is my mother, emerging from the bedroom and going into the bathroom. She is leaving this afternoon to visit her friend in Toronto, and I'm a little sad. But she will stop here again for two or three days on her way home.

The radio, as every morning, is playing, and, after several days of sunshine, the sky is blue-gray, and it looks like rain. Britain and Argentina are still at it over the Falkland Islands, and America and Russia mention nuclear war too often. And, more importantly at the moment: I'm starting a two-week assignment at Bankers Trust as proofreader, and it occurs to me that I don't need a fulltime job, I can continue with my proofing at the law firm and taking on short assignments to supplement my income. Decision made, and time to rise and kiss my mother and make her breakfast and help her pack and take her to the airport. I know that we will try very hard not to cry, and that we will cry, we always do.

And Dorothy just came in with a homemade loaf of nut bread, and she'll join mama et moi for coffee and breakfast!

Two nights ago I dreamt that I watch M. cut his wedding ring with scissors. The ring gave in easily, like it was made of plastic. Cheap! And useless. I, of course, put my ring away a long time ago, and hopefully the promise I made my mother will soon be fact.

And now to Bankers Trust that has turned out to be a dream-job, the people are super friendly and the atmosphere relaxed, quite different from the law firm where everyone seems harried and tense most of the time. Till later.

After an invigorating weekend in Bear Mountain-Harriman State Park with Lucy and Emma and their friends. Fresh air, and trees, and hiking, and sitting and talking around the campfire late into the night in the woods near Lake Welch. In the morning we jumped into the lake, but couldn't stay in too long, it was freeeezing. And today caught up with myself, reading the book reviews I hadn't had time to read these past few weeks, and now, having immersed myself reading about writing and writers, I find that I share their fears and doubts but not their output and productivity. No magic here: people who work produce.

And now, alone again, facing the daily future, a mild melancholy. I tell myself that I'm not really happy, but then I also tell myself there's no such thing as "constant happy," so what I lack is deep and basic contentment and a safety-net peace of mind. On the whole, I enjoy what I do, I have good moments, but fundamentally, I think, a vague restlessness gnaws at me. Possibly because I feel I'm not doing enough, I'm not as productive as I'd like to be. I've worked out a new schedule whereby I commit to work every day—even on days when I have to go to work—at least three hours a day. I'll report my failings here to see what kind of excuses I use to avoid work.

And, before I leave you, here's D.H. Lawrence, restoring my confidence re plot-making: "Anyhow, I don't want a plot, I should be bored with it."

My friends and I were among the crazy few who ventured out with food and expectations to listen to the Philharmonic in the park. Crazy because it rained most of the morning and rain was predicted for the evening/night, but we went anyway, deciding that the forecast would be proven wrong and that the concert would take place as scheduled. And, as soon as we reached the park around 6pm, it started to rain, not a hard rain, more of a drizzle, but steady enough to drench us to the point where it didn't matter anymore. We spread our blankets and brought out the food and talked and exchanged jokes with the people around us.

The orchestra was there also, on the stage (they, at least, were protected by the band shell), and we all waited for the rain to stop. It didn't, and so, at 7:45 the orchestra spokesman regretfully announced that it can't be done, the instruments are delicate and don't like rain. They were ready and willing to play, but nature said no. We rose to our feet and applauded as we watched them leave, then finished our dinner-picnic of cheese, bread, Chinese noodles, and wine, and then packed our things and left, and here I am in the living room, now dry and content.

My sister is on her way to California, my mother is in Canada, and I am here, at my desk, looking over a few rejection slips, which, so far for "Vaseline," have been encouraging, handwritten personal notes, like this one from Redbook: "This is nicely written, but not a must for us. Please let us see more of your work." Maybe this is the process every writer has to endure: first cold form-letter rejections, then friendlier, handwritten notes, and then, hopefully, an acceptance?

Divorce is not easy, and I'll have to go through it. I met M. tonight and it was mostly bad: bad feelings, discomfort, resentment. We saw a movie—"Porky's"—a movie he raved about, a movie that left me cold. But that's not all. We went to the bar where his friend Leo works and had dinner and argued about the film. Then we transcended it, and were tender with one another for a while, as if for old times' sake.

I can hardly move the pen on the page, not so much because of alcohol, but mostly because I'm cold and stiff, and also maybe a little drunk, not really drunk, but I did have a three drinks tonight, which is to be expected if you spend time with a drinker in a bar, and this is one of the reasons I did what I did tonight. And here it is. M. put me in a cab and said he'd call in half an hour to make sure I got home all right. I got home all right, and was already in bed, reading while waiting for the promised call so he doesn't wake me up later on. But the call never came.

I got out of bed, angrier than the devil, but still willing to give M. the benefit of doubt. I called Leo's bar and, sure enough, M. was there, giving me an excuse, a feeble one, about people who came into the bar and they started talking, and that's why he didn't call, but he was going to, it was on his mind. I told him I don't like myself around him, I don't want him to call me anymore, I want a divorce, I've had it. Now, I think, the devil in me has shrunk and I feel like myself again, even relieved: the words I've wanted to say for so long, have been said, and the actual deed will follow.

And, as I sit here, thinking about this useless, time-wasting aggravation, I also realize that, in a strange way, he interferes with my very being. When I'm with him, I actually feel distanced from myself, he alienates me from myself, from my sense of existing in the world. When he's around, I feel alienated from everything around me, I become inert, numb. But, no more! And now back to bed and slowly calm myself with the help of Raymond Queneau's *Exercises in Style*, and then a well-deserved, restful sleep.

Strange, strange, strange. I'm going through a difficult and strange period. I keep reminding myself that I must embrace my solitude and concentrate on work. Live my life, allowing no time for complaints, gripes, but be satisfied with the occasional joy of accomplishment and keep the pen moving, as I'm doing now. I must relearn to live and appreciate the moment, the simple fact that I'm alive.

Night. Breezy. Rousing trumpets from radio. Bright lamp overhead, and willing quiet to spread in my heart, my brain. Earlier today, during the morning rush hour, I saw a young woman hailing a cab, a baby held in her arm, its sleepy face in the nook of her shoulder and neck, the folded stroller resting against her hip, as she hailed a cab with her free hand—what confidence, toughness, in her movements; a tigress fending for herself and her baby.

It's early morning, 4am, and here after a wild night of fun and dancing. And yes, I've had a few drinks, but my head is clear. The evening started with dinner at Emma's—delicious—and then the four of us—Pia, Lucy, Emma, and I—went to the Mudd Club. The main attraction: each to his own on the dance floor, live and let live. You can be as wild as your heart permits, which is great, and possibly too great: everyone is so busy doing their own thing, they don't notice the other. No communication. Individualized individuals, shadows in the dark, "empty" to their surroundings and to themselves. It's fun for a night, but as a regular diet too insular and strangely oppressive.

And, something that's been on my mind for a while but never wrote it down here: friends who know M., or people who met him, however briefly, they all say the same thing: I'm outgoing, alive, an "emotional bomb," as Emma said tonight, while he's an introvert, a "cold fish." How did the two of us ever get together? Compared to me he's an iceberg, and I come from the desert. It doesn't really matter anymore, but interesting to hear it from people.

And, it's time to say goodnight. I hear garbage trucks humming downstairs. It's a new day, and night as well, but I'm wide awake, excited with life. I'd better rise from this desk and go to bed and try to get some sleep.

11pm. Back from the Berkshires, a peaceful weekend by the lake, pleasing the eye and soothing the spirit.

And tomorrow another week begins, a week of work, of running around, of taking care of everyday errands. Do I let time pass, or do I actively participate in life?

This morning, by the lake, a small black poodle was lured into the water by his owners. The dog went in, not enthusiastically, and swam a little, and then got out and stood on the sand, watching the boy and girl who were waving their arms and calling, trying to lure him back into the water. But he bravely resisted their calls, saying, don't push it, guys. I came in to accommodate your wishes, but enough is enough, I'm not coming in again. Not today. I totally empathized with the dog because I, too, wouldn't go into the heart-stopping cold water.

And now it is really time for bed, and tomorrow back to the week's rhythmic grind.

The big moment is here, I'm finally back at my desk, about to take a fresh look at my stories in progress, and this after a busy week, two part-time jobs, friends, neighbors, food shopping, cleaning, and the rest of it. And it's a bright Saturday morning, and many things have been rambling in my head, thoughts, questions, sparks of realizations, possibilities, things that strike me for one reason or another but are not always committed to paper. Many of these sparks take place on the bus on my way to work, or when with friends and something they say strikes a note in my brain, and then, if striking enough, remains in brain, oftentimes for always.

And, most important: brought my short stories to a creative writing professor at Columbia University, and there's a chance I'll get a scholarship to join his writing workshop. Next Wednesday I'll be meeting him again and have a definite answer, yes or no, re the scholarship; this is the first time I'm applying for one. He'll go over my stories before he decides, and I pray he finds what he's looking for, not only because of the workshop, but because it will boost my confidence. I'm eager to go back to school, and even daydream that he'd offer me an assistantship, so that I can quit the jobs and find myself among people who do what I do, people who value reciprocity.

Such a good and pleasant day today. I worked well, and now outside the window an afternoon hour that feels soft and romantic. Obviously, I'm in great spirits, listening to records I used to listen to nonstop a few years ago, and this past week they found their way out of the pile and onto the stereo, going round and round: Marvin Gaye, Carole King, Jackson Browne, Crosby, Stills & Nash. Am I nostalgic for the time I met and then moved in and lived with M.? No, just enjoying the moment, the music. And, if I do feel nostalgic, it is nostalgia for the person I was before I ever met M.

Labor Day Weekend is here. A year or so ago, M. went uptown to look for himself. It seems amazing, but this year really flew in and out in a hurry, with me holding onto its wings. And tomorrow morning I'm leaving for East Hampton with Jamie and taking my stories along. Jamie, too, is determined to get some work done.

Back home from East Hampton where I spent a peaceful and interesting weekend with Jamie and her mother. Interesting thanks, in part, to Jamie's mother and her friends— accomplished women in their late fifties-early sixties, secure in their place in society. Sitting around and listening to them talk, I marveled, with a mixture of envy and admiration, at their confident manner, their middle-age solidity. On the whole, we didn't "do" much, it felt good to be lazy. We ate well, went to the beach or lay on the grass, and talked a lot about writing, books, the midterm elections. Here are a couple of notes I jotted down in my room:

Rachel (Jamie's mother's friend): "The entrenched notion that women are whiners, never happy and content with their lot, is of course a myth created by those who believe they carry a God-given treasure, usually small, in their pants." (Everyone cracks up.) "It must be said that it is the male in our midst who has always been the better and more accomplished noise-maker. Success, as he sees it, is his birthright. Women should step aside and be quiet."

"Smokers are pensive," Jamie says and I watch as she takes a long and deep draw. For a moment, her face partially disappears behind a fog of smoke rising from her mouth and nostrils, and I, mesmerized, watch and wait for Jamie's face to reappear. I like it when she comes up with such pronouncements, often out of the blue, because afterward she says nothing, and then my brain gets to work, wondering what she is thinking, how far she travels, and if she is waiting for me to respond.

On the train back home, I was thinking about this journal, regretting not having started long ago, fifteen or more years ago, recording my thoughts and all that was happening with me, in my head, when I was in my teens, or even earlier. I have a general feeling/notion about who I was when growing up. I remember friends and teachers, I remember specific interactions, incidents, good and not so good. I remember reading books, but I have no mental conception of the person I was, no specific memories of what I was thinking, and what I was hoping for the future, except the desire to be a grownup already. I believe that fundamentally I'm the same person I was, but I can't be sure. It would have been interesting and gratifying to open a notebook now and read what was going on in my head years ago, and relieve what went on in my life, my inner life, at the time. And this has nothing to do with being a writer, but simply with being alive and aware. I almost can't wait for twenty years to pass, to a time when I will open this book and reconnect with myself as I read these words.

And, good to be back at my desk, in my bed and duvet, my shower, and cooking a meal in my kitchen, where the nose, too, benefits, thanks to turmeric and lemongrass and lots of garlic. And, of course, back to you, back to work. Routine is the most reliable pacifier.

Best news ever! I went to Columbia University and met again with Humphreys of the creative writing program who told me that I got the scholarship, and that I'll be the "star of the class" because I have "a good sense of rhythm." I'm totally beside myself with joy! I'm a student again, and next week classes begin.

And my mother is here, back from Canada. She'll be staying a few days, and I'm patient and caring, a stranger would say: a model daughter!

And Pia left a few minutes ago. She came over and we rewrote a letter she wants to send to E.L. Doctorow about his novel *The Book of Daniel.*

And now, again, it's time for bed. I'm a bit nervous but also excited about being a student again, in a writing workshop at a university considered one of the best in the country. Am I a writer after all? Focus. I need a sharp, focused lens in my brain, and discipline in my bones. That's all I need. It sounds simple and obvious right now, but, at times, everything is difficult and muddled.

I'm super excited about Columbia, and also proud. A couple of months ago I set out to enroll in this workshop, and I did. I hope it's a good class that will give me the structure and discipline I need.

I like these quiet moments with myself, closing off the day, getting ready for tomorrow, listening to street noises, the radio, and the constant hum of my fish tank.

Saw my mother off and if the flight left on time she's up there now, over the ocean, maybe wiping a tear. We both cried in the cab on the way to the airport, calmed down as two adults should, and cried again when time came to say goodbye before she boarded. We're both so overwrought when we're together, and it's unclear if we cry because we fear this is the last time we see each other, or because we regret that we don't get along better, or because we both hide our feelings from each other and feel bad for it. Watching her march up the ramp, a small, resolute figure, I cried some more, and then again on the bus, going back to the city.

Now I'm calm, and the thought comes that from now on I must seclude myself more and work harder—we have to bring a story a week to the workshop—but then a counter thought winks, as if to remind me that the more you seclude yourself, the more detached you are from life around you, the more room for megalomania to set in.

Back from Columbia, from my first night in class, and I'm excited like a kid about the reading (*Colossus* by Henry Miller) and writing assignments. Well, not exactly like a kid, if I were still a kid I'd grumble, Oh, too much homework, but here I am, saying, Oh, yes, give me more.

And, a decision made tonight: socializing will have to wait, and therefore I won't leave town this weekend and will cancel camping plans. From now on it's work and productivity. I have to devote myself and become a fanatic. I'm full of life again, hopeful with plans and goals, and also confidence about—and here I'm going to use a big word—my vocation.

John Gardner is dead, killed in a motorcycle accident, and Grace Kelly is dead after a car accident. Awful stories out of Lebanon: the massacre in two Palestinian refugee camps, Sabra and Shatila, in West Beirut. The Israelis didn't pull the trigger, Lebanese Christian militias did, but they were there, at the site of the massacres. Were they ordered not to interfere and allow the killings to take place? The Israelis claim they didn't hear/see anything. Is this possible? They had surrounded the camps and must have heard the shootings and the screams. I don't know what to think anymore. Does Begin believe that Israel is immune to criticism, and that the world will forever accept the image of the Israeli soldier as a hero of peace? I should stop listening to the news. It warps my mind, my thinking, and squeezes my heart.

Last night second Columbia class, and except for five minutes of a silly discussion— initiated by one of the students—about libel suits (!) the class was good and engaging. On my way home, I scribbled this note:

Am on the bus after second Columbia class, and I think I've got the answer to a dilemma I've been trying to pinpoint for a long time. Sitting on the bus, thinking about voice, tone—subjects we discussed in class—I realize that my main problem is that I often don't allow my natural voice to emerge. When I do allow it, the writing is free and flowing, alive with humor, but when I block my voice and pretend to be someone else, someone who is clever and cynical—a façade to cover a trembling, insecure being—the writing feels forced, lifeless. I mustn't try to be "original" and different; this should happen naturally if the voice is true. I should definitely work more and let spontaneity take over, instead of premeditating and editorializing.

I remember watching Asimov giving an interview and saying, quite simply, that in the morning he gets up, sits at the typewriter, and begins typing whatever comes to his head, allowing words to come and roll and play and something eventually happens, something begins to develop. Viewed from this angle, I can say that I approach the work too somberly, too "reverently." I should allow myself more room, more freedom, more FUN, let my mind play games, and, above all, be faithful to and trust myself, and everything else will fall into place.

And now Placido Domingo is singing an aria from "Rigoletto" and I sit and think about my work, my solitude. This morning, preparing breakfast, I decided that a writer's work is more trying than the work of any other artist. Painters get their hands dirty. They deal with colors, smelling them, mixing them, deriving sensual and mental pleasure from the mere act of moving brush over canvas, watching it change before their eyes. The same is true of sculptors, who also deal with matter and get their hands dirty. Musicians and composers deal with sounds, they play an instrument that responds to them. A writer works with words, everyday words that at times may feel empty, overused, and the writer somehow needs to transform and elevate them, make them sing and reverberate, make them adhere, turn an abstraction into something that's tangible and alive. Enough philosophizing. Work!

11:30pm. Let me congratulate myself. Wrote the first draft of "Miranda," a short story for class, needs two-three more drafts, not bad at all as first draft, it has a slant to it that I like.

October is here, and so is summer weather, still lingering. People, expecting winter to arrive any minute, dress accordingly and therefore suffocate all day in too heavy clothes. I certainly do.

This month, eight years ago, I arrived in New York, a wide-eyed gamine, and, looking back, I'm happy to conclude that I did accomplish a lot—in the main: I've developed into a person. I wrote a novel and put it in a drawer to hibernate and to be resurrected in the future when I'm better equipped for it. I write short stories and collect rejection slips. I've made friends, I got married, separated, and life is wide open still. And, nothing to sneeze at: I support myself without a helpmeet.

And, good work today on "Roughing It on Fire Island" for my next class assignment: write about someone you know without expressing an opinion. I was trying, for the past few days, to write about my mother, but opinions and explanations kept creeping in. Then I wrote about Jamie and her efforts to instruct me in the art of flirting, but only came up with a few sentences, probably because I didn't take to heart any of her "tips" and didn't put them to use. And then I remembered "Roughing It," about the Fire Island camping trip with Lucy and Emma, a story I began a while ago, and today sat down to work and develop it, and I think it works: it is all description, no opinions, no explanations. I retyped another draft, and tomorrow will retype it again and submit. It'll be interesting to hear what Humphreys says about its unconventional structure, about its incantation-like repetitions. It's really a kind of a long poem, in prose. Ready for bed again, with *Home Truths*—a book of short stories by the one and only Mavis Gallant.

My buzzer just rang, and my heart is pounding—who can be buzzing me at this hour? My immediate thought was: Bob, who stopped here last night on his way to L.A., but it can't be him since his plane left this afternoon. Probably a mistake.

And, nearly forgot! In the mail tonight my student I.D. card arrived, and the photo I.D., taken right there at the Columbia admissions office, is so telling: my face is a glowing smile, I look healthy, full of life, and happy, the image of someone who's about to embark on a long and wonderful journey.

I'm in trouble again today, restless, discouraged, and questioning myself, and this always happens when I feel I'm not productive enough. I begin to weigh and examine my life, my future, and see no progress. Many questions and doubts, and no ready answers. Tomorrow and tomorrow, said the poet. But I have to stop whining and get a hold of myself.

But it's also possible that something is brewing in me, maybe a new story, maybe my brain is trying to figure something out before involving me, and therefore I'm feeling restless. I may be deluding myself, but if delusion helps, delusion is good. Work will tell.

I am. Came here to report that I'm feeling much much better. Worked all afternoon and finally managed to get down the piece about my mother, not for class, but for myself, and I'm glad it came out well, not only without opinions, but also tender, paying her tribute, giving her credit, long overdue. When it's done and typed, I'll send it to her, and I can only hope she'll accept it as an apology for my awful past behavior. I did try to apologize to her over the telephone a few days ago, and she told me to forget it, let bygones be bygones, words that surprised and overwhelmed me.

And now, thanks to good work, I'm back to my usual energetic self. I believe in and like myself again, until the next "brewing." Tomorrow and Sunday—work! And now to my comfy bed.

Cleaned the apartment, then myself, had breakfast, read, and now here, getting ready for a full workday. Placido and Pavarotti on the stereo, clouds in sky promise rain, and an American flag is blowing in the wind atop the building across the street. Yesterday, a note in the mail from M. telling me he loves me. Indeed. What is love?

The sun emerges from under a cloud, and I'm in a philosophical mood this morning. I wonder how many writers sit at their desks right now, working, while the rest of humanity enjoys a day of leisure, going on trips with family and kids, reading the paper, paying bills, mowing the lawn, washing the car, going out shopping for food and other necessities.

And, found a great poem for you about a marriage that was. It's a short poem by Yehuda Amichai, translated by Assia Gutmann, who killed herself on account of Ted Hughes, using the same method as Sylvia, turning on the gas oven, except that Assia, unlike Sylvia, did not spare the child she had with Hughes, four-year-old Shura, but chose to take the child with her. I can't imagine what such a decision entails.

I found this small volume of *Selected Poems* in the Strand, and the title of the poem is "A Pity. We Were Such a Good Invention." Here are the last two stanzas:

A pity. We were such a good
And loving invention.
An aeroplane made from a man and wife.
Wings and everything.
We hovered a little above the earth.

We even flew a little.

Later. 11:30pm. Worked all day, nowhere—wow, meant to write: now here, and, in my haste, left no space, to realize that "now here" can easily become "nowhere." And so, now here, closing off another precious day and night. Lea called earlier, asking if I want to see "Cats," she has an extra ticket, and I had to say no because the ticket is for Tuesday, and I have class on Tuesday. Also had to give up Herbert Von Karajan who will be in New York next week for four performances. I bought a ticket months ago, but gave my ticket to Pia because Karajan, too, falls on a Tuesday. I find myself foregoing things I love without the slightest hesitation: school comes first.

A quiet Saturday night. Was supposed to ring Emma and meet, or ring Jamie and meet, but I find myself, find myself, find myself not wanting to go out, want to stay home and read, work, or watch a film on TV, which I did tonight for the first time in I don't know how long, watched "Hands Across the Table," an old romantic comedy that kindled a brief romantic yearning in me for a warm and loving touch as I watched the characters kiss on the screen. And I let out a sigh, half-mocking myself, and thinking: Will I ever meet love again, solid and passionate and no inhibitions? Am I turning into a teenager again?

Earlier, thinking about Humphreys, I went back to when he first told me that I had a good sense of rhythm (he also mentioned this in class a couple of times), when I kind of understood what he meant, but now I have a better sense of it, and I notice that, when I work on a story or when I read it to myself, I become aware of my heartbeat, and, even more pronounced, I feel that my upper body is in motion, moving back and forth with the rhythm of the words, almost like a davening Jew in temple. Interesting to suddenly recognize something I hadn't been aware of until Humphreys drew my attention to it.

It is 1am., and mid-Manhattan is clear, says the radio. A woman was acquitted after putting a knife through her estranged husband's heart, father of her five children. And the FBI found fingerprints on one of the Tylenol bottles whose capsules were laced with cyanide. A crazy business this Tylenol affair, which touched off a few other crazy copycats, such as acid in mouthwash and Visine—imagine the malice and hate!

Another day is almost over, and I see it off with a glass of wine and a cigarette. And then to bed and book. And another page filled with words.

Ten minutes after midnight, and here I am again after another night in class. I feel that I'm learning, that my mind is expanding, even though precious time is sometimes wasted on "shop talk," basically when a student asks a question, such as: Can you tell us the difference in writers' pay-scale on Broadway and Hollywood (unbelievable!), and a long discussion ensues, and Humphreys, too gentle to stop it, lets himself be sidetracked, and I stifle a scream, but do show my discontent by audibly sighing and shifting in my seat.

Last night I woke up in the middle of the night, or, I think I woke myself up so I can control the desired progression and happy conclusion to what had started as a magical dream where I meet this man with whom intellectual, emotional, and sexual relationship develops. Lying in bed half awake half asleep, I told myself to stop this nonsense and fall asleep, but of course I didn't listen and continued to cling to the all-consuming idyllic images. I remember how the dream began: I'm sitting in the middle of the Great Lawn in Central Park, it's evening, and we're a group of friends waiting for a concert to begin, and suddenly I notice this stranger in our midst and the attraction is instant and mutual.

Ah, well. And now to bed again, to more dreams, hopes, disappointments, and the usual back and forth.

1:30am. And it's also 2:30am, because the clock moved back for DST, and I'm home after a Halloween party at Becky's. I wore a homemade costume of what I hoped will look like a Can-Can dancer, but a few people thought it was an Apache costume! Pia went all out and arrived as an elegant tall banana. There were many other amazing costumes, and again I marveled at these enterprising Americans who take their costume-making seriously, rather than putting together a costume in a minute, which, needless to say, is what I did. Next year I'll invest more time and effort.

I didn't do any real work today but read and thought about writing. I did clean the apartment, though, which is also satisfying when finished and done with. Tomorrow will be all work and no excuses. Today I also visited Lucia, a neighbor's daughter who is in hospital after an asthma attack, and, in another room, I saw a little girl strapped to a wheelchair and crying. She was crying when I got there, wailing, and was still crying when I left, not wailing anymore, but whimpering. There was no one in her room, a little girl alone, crying in a wheelchair, and no one coming in to check on her. I wanted to go into her room and talk to her but was afraid she'd cry even harder.

On the bus, coming home from the party, I glanced at an old woman's watch and it said 2:10; apparently, she forgot to move the time back an hour. For her, time moves forward only. Late night brings out the philosopher in me, which, I'm sure, is a sign that it's time for bed with William Trevor's short stories.

I love these quiet hours, classical music on the radio, and me, sitting at my desk, thoroughly relaxed, letting my thoughts take over, not intense thoughts, but just promenading thoughts. I even told myself in the mirror that I liked myself. Sometimes doubts overwhelm me, but not tonight.

Did good work today and finished a second draft of "Snow," a poem I began two weeks ago on the bus, coming home from class. I think it's a good poem, it's simple and direct, and I like it. Then I got myself out of the house and went uptown to the 92nd Street Y and listened to John Guare and David Mamet read their work. Guare read excerpts from different plays, including *Muzeeka*. He was magnificent, his writing lively, poetic, original. Then Mamet and his director read a short one-act—a work-in-progress—and tonight was its first public reading. It's titled: "The Disappearance of Jews" and it is simple, funny, and direct. I was hoping there will be a discussion, but instead they had a reception with wine and playwrights signing autographs. I hesitated before going up to them with the program in my hand for them to sign. I've never asked for an autograph before and am not a worshipper. But I finally did go up to them because I wanted to ask Mamet if writing dialogue comes easy to him; it sounds like it does. I went up to him and asked him, and the answer was yes, it's easy for him, and that's why it sounds easy. An honest, spontaneous reply, but I was a bit surprised, I thought he'd give me the usual spiel about how hard it is to write, but he didn't. He smiled and said it comes easy to him. I wanted to tell him that I envied him but didn't.

Then Guare, too, signed my program and, as he signed it, I thought about "Lydie Breeze" but, of course, said nothing. And now, here I am, reporting on it and also attaching the program to the back of this book. Also extraordinary to witness tonight was the love of the audience for the writers and the heartfelt response of the writers to this love.

I read a great poem today, Theodore Roethke's "Open House," doubly poignant for me because I often feel I'm too much of an open house. Roethke says, "Myself is what I wear:/I keep the spirit spare."

And now, good night.

Met Pia tonight and, again, a full and rich night, we always have things to say to one another, conversation flows, associations fly, and brains are present. We also saw a special, moving film, "Céleste," a German-made film about Proust and Céleste—his maid, and much more. A unique and absorbing masterpiece based on the book Céleste herself wrote. Later, Pia and I talked and talked, about the film, about husbands, estranged husbands, lovers, life experiences, love songs, romanticism—dead or alive, and here I am, ready to go to bed, tired but not tired, and tomorrow to the office, and then the weekend and a different kind of work, my work.

These past two days, I've been thinking about writing a story about my French father, Simonil, a story I could read in class. Simonil who was like a father to me, and the story will open with my first question to him when I came to his restaurant that served kosher food for students in Paris. It was in the morning, when the restaurant was not open yet. I didn't know this at the time, but it was open only for lunch and dinner, and you needed a special student voucher to be served. I went there after someone gave me the address and told me it was a government-subsidized restaurant for students, and that it was cheap, a franc and a half for a five-course meal.

When I arrived at the address, the restaurant was closed. In fact, it didn't even look like a restaurant, and, as I stood there, confused and disappointed, I saw this short, stocky, powerfully built man hauling crates of vegetables from a van at the curb and into the restaurant. After watching him go back and forth between van and restaurant, I summoned the courage to approach him, and stopped him as he walked from the van toward the restaurant.

"Êtes-vous juif?" I asked, and he glared at me for what seemed like a very long time. (Later on I learned that "juif" had pejorative connotations; "Israelite" was the proper usage.) He then put the crate down on the pavement, pulled up his shirt and showed me the tassels of his tallit. This brought a big smile of gratitude and relief to my lips, and this is how he became my father and the restaurant my home and refuge, where I had my lunch and dinner, where I sat with him in his office a few mornings a week and talked about this and that, and where he let me taste pastries he'd just baked, all of them mouthwatering.

When I needed help or advice or to borrow money until my allowance arrived, he was the one I turned to. The restaurant was on the small Rue de Médicis, across the street from the Luxembourg Gardens, and right in the center of the Latin Quarter. Indeed, my home and refuge, and in my heart still as if only a few days passed since I left Paris and came here.

Tonight met M. for dinner, a stormy one at first, but then we both calmed down, and now it's done: we agreed that divorce is the only option for us. Of course we added the obligatory and hopeful "we'll remain friends" and I think we both meant it. We do feel a bit of regret, tinged with fondness, we were young when we met, and things change, people change, we've changed, and life goes on. Now that we've made the decision and voiced it, it feels as though we're both relieved, and certainly calmer, maybe even, finally, reconciled adults. Or something close to adults. Amen and Hallelujah!

And now Verdi's "Nabuco" on the record player, and sometimes the pen assumes a life of its own, and I continue scribbling with the music in my head, and the music from the stereo. My writing occupies me more and more. I'm no longer afraid of it, and I'm finally taking myself seriously, but not too seriously. I'm growing up, while also remaining the child I feel I still am, accepting life and always marveling at the miracle of it. I know it and I live it every day, with the miracle but also with the fear that we, humanity, will self-destruct one day with the help of weak men. And so, the impulse is to hold onto life, every minute of it, and concentrate on pleasure, ephemeral, but also real while it lasts, both the mental and the physical. I'm getting philosophical again, so it's time for bed. This has been a good and consequential day. Calm reigns in my heart.

Great excitement this morning in the park. A huge hawk up in a tree—some people saying there are two of them, husband and wife—gray and majestic and awe-inspiring. Humans gather and gawk and point, pigeons and squirrels, the usual residents, are troubled, jolted from their usual peaceful existence. The pigeons, I guess, have flown away to safer parts. Most of the squirrels have gone into hiding, except for a few who stand guard on their hind legs, emitting cries of distress/ warning, hoping their collective front will frighten and discourage the invaders/ intruders and persuade them to continue on their way—this park belongs to its regular residents!

Later. Back from a second visit to the park to report that the hawks must have left and gone south. The pigeons and squirrels are celebrating, doubly energetic, joyous, and industrious. On the way home: a group of Chinese men and women, old and emaciated, collecting and counting bagfuls of empty cans and bottles—a new industry of the poor. And yesterday, crossing the street, a black man pushing a cartful of blue plastic bags bursting with cans and bottles, and man and cart seemed like a moving blue mountain of crests and ridges.

I am. Spent all day indoors except for a quick outing for food and newspaper, and read and wrote all day and watched the news while devouring steak with mushrooms and broccoli, and, of course, salad and Italian bread, and then a pear and raisins, and suddenly I felt something strange happening to my vision, like an electric charge, as if the TV rays extended out of the TV screen into my right eye, and since this funny feeling lasted quite a while I began to worry, thinking that something was the matter with my vision, possibly permanent damage, but then the funny sensation vanished, and all was normal again.

This odd experience brought on the memory of the half-dream-half-awake "dybbuk" that seemed to have entered my body and made it levitate toward the window. I guess this is what people who live alone experience once in a while, especially people like me who dwell all day in contemplation, removed and detached from others. Being alone doesn't bother me, I don't think, I don't even realize that I am "alone" until something strange happens, as if to remind me of the delicate balance between "normal" and—what? "abnormal"? Some chemical combination or reaction suddenly dominates, and our "sane" "programmed" "organized" brain is momentarily rattled.

I'm fine now, except for a mild headache and sensitivity in the eyes; I do strain my eyes and I'd better take better care of them. And soon to bed and book and tomorrow another week of living and laughing and deep and profound happiness, affection, warmth, honesty.

And here, to close, a few words from Joni Mitchell's new album. I haven't heard it yet but read about it in the paper:

People don't know how to love
They taste it and toss it
Turn it off and on
Like a bathtub faucet

All in all I'm leading a healthy, safe life, no major risks, no extremes of ups and downs. A peaceful existence of day in and day out, work at the office, work at my desk, and, on good days, a daily diet of five cigarettes—am now smoking my fifth and last for the day.

Today was a bit unusual, felt tired all day and the headache from a few nights ago is still with me, off and on, I may be more exhausted than I know, so I'll take an aspirin now and go to bed—it's 8:30pm!—with Brecht's play "In the Jungle of Cities," and tomorrow is Tuesday, annual checkup in the morning, class with Humphreys in the evening, day in and day out, calm and peaceful, even if sometimes I feel that I don't really live but am more like a spirit flitting in and out of buses, offices, apartments. Only the weather changes, and days of the week.

Lately, night after night, I've been waking up remembering my dreams, but not bothering to write them down. And then I forget them. I do remember one because it involves taking off my shirt in the office and, since I don't wear a bra, I walk around the office bare-chested. I feel a bit embarrassed, but I don't put my shirt back on. I don't know why I take off my shirt, maybe it's warm in the office, at any rate, I don't remember if there's a compelling reason for me to take off my shirt, or if it's a natural, spontaneous act.

It's not the first time that I dream that I take off my clothes in public: sometimes I'm stark naked. I know that Freud and Jung had something to say about nakedness in dreams, something to do with shame/guilt, or the opposite, no shame at all.

I'm now in bed, after my shower, with coffee and cigarette and you, and it's foggy outside, and it's another Monday morning. And soon to the office.

Midnight. I was cooped up in the apartment all day, reading and working, so I didn't realize that spring weather had arrived, if only for a day. In the evening I went out and met Jamie, we had a delicious falafel dinner at Mamoun's on MacDougal Street, and then saw *The Return of the Secaucus Seven*, a film that could easily have been self-indulgent about the glorious sixties, but it wasn't, it was well written and acted and, in parts, really funny. No "action" or plot, just good dialogue that sustained and held the movie together.

This book is approaching its end, and a new year will roll around soon with its 365 new days, to be recorded in a new book, and please, not too many instances of despair to plunge me into deep waters and no lifeboat. And it is dark outside, and all is quiet and still, and here I begin to race against the last empty page of this notebook, writing with an urgency and speed that bring to mind the survivor in *One Hundred Years of Solitude*—the ending of which is one of the most thrilling and memorable passages in literature. I read it about ten years ago and still remember it vividly, the image of myself reading the last paragraph when the survivor is reading about the end of his world, and he realizes in a flash that when he's finished reading his end will come, but he can't stop and he keeps on reading, just like the fascinated reader who holds her breath and continues reading till she reaches the last word on the page—what was that last word?—but what a marvelous way to end a book, an unstoppable onward plunge, and this García Márquez, who's getting the Nobel Prize next month, brought to life on paper the essence of life, in that we can't stop the course of life events, of Time, it's a blind force, an energy that pulls us onward, allowing no "time" to catch our breaths, pulls us onward toward our inevitable last breaths, but, in the mean"time" we create, we eat, we remember, we mourn and celebrate, we love and hate and, joyful and sorrowful, we go on, even if, like Gogo, we sometimes say, I can't go on, and we do go on because we can't and don't really want to stop, and here we've arrived at the end of the page, the last line, and it now occurs to me that the name Gogo may suggest Go go don't stop

About the Author

Tsipi Keller was born in Prague, raised in Israel, studied in Paris, and now lives in the US. Novelist and translator, she is the author of fourteen books, and the recipient of several literary awards, including National Endowment for the Arts Translation Fellowships, and New York Foundation for the Arts Fiction Awards. Her fiction is often characterized as literary, urban, noir, and her work has been compared to the work of Jean Rhys, Kate Chopin, Edith Wharton, and Patricia Highsmith. Her latest novel, *Nadja on Nadja*, was published by Underground Voices.

About the Press

Unsolicited Press is a small press in Portland, Oregon. The publisher produces fiction, poetry, and creative nonfiction written by emerging and award-winning authors.

Learn more at unsolicitedpress.com.

CPSIA information can be obtained
at www.ICGtesting.com
Printed in the USA
LVHW042344130920
665903LV00003B/721